MW00561862

Middle School Teacher Plans and Resources for
A Land Remembered: Student Edition

Margaret Sessions Paschal

Pineapple Press, Inc.
Sarasota, Florida

Middle School Teacher Plans and Resources
for *A Land Remembered: Student Edition*
by Patrick D. Smith

Copyright © 2005 by Margaret Sessions Paschal

All rights reserved.

ISBN-13: 978-1-56164-341-7
ISBN-10: 1-56164-341-6

Published by:

Pineapple Press, Inc.
P.O. Box 3889
Sarasota, Florida 34230

www.pineapplepress.com

All parts of this manual may be photocopied for classroom use.

About the cover: Cover photograph by Judge Nelson Bailey shows Dewaine Hazellief on a marshtackie with cur dogs on a Florida cow hunt.

Table of Contents

Volume 1 1863–1880

Volume 2 1880–1968

Author's Preface

As a native Floridian and educator, I have found the writing and implementation of these lesson plans very gratifying. It has been a joy for me to hear the positive comments of my students and see their excitement and anticipation as we prepare to read each chapter. I hear them discussing *A Land Remembered* in the hallways and catch them reading ahead. One of my favorite memories as a teacher is an incident in which one of my students told a friend of hers who was not in my class about our study of the book. Her friend was so interested she bought a book of her own. It is my prayer that continued teaching of the book will generate responses like this, which will surely help our beautiful state avoid becoming a land remembered, but instead remain a land revered for and preserved in its natural beauty for all Floridians and their descendants.

For information on Margaret Paschal's availability to speak on the use of these lesson plans at teacher training sessions, please contact Pineapple Press. (Contact information is available on the copyright page in the front of the book.)

Introduction

Florida Challenges and Choices is included in the eighth grade curriculum of the school where I teach. Since we have no textbook for this class, I use the student volumes of *A Land Remembered* since it encompasses the history of the state—and does it in a way that generates high interest for my students. The story begins with the Civil War and its impact on Florida and ends with the impact of urbanization in the 1960s, including the influx of immigrants from Latin America and the Miami race riots of 1968.

The book and the lesson plans are not only excellent resources for teaching the history of the state of Florida, but are also invaluable tools in creating awareness in young people of the many ecosystems in the state that are threatened by residential and business development. Once they become environmentally conscious, my students are truly able to see their surroundings through "new eyes."

These lesson plans divide each chapter into four sections: Vocabulary/Slang, Pre-reading Activities, Comprehension Questions, and Post-reading Activities.

The **Vocabulary/Slang words** are listed in sequential order as they appear in the chapter. (Note: When I have included the counted paragraph location for finding words or text on a page I include the first paragraph at the top of the page in my count even if it is not a complete paragraph.) The meaning of the Vocabulary/Slang words should be considered prior to reading the chapter. Whether you choose to do this through oral discussion or a paper-and-pencil lesson will depend on the reading ability and experience of your students and your classroom time constraints.

The purpose of the **Pre-reading Activities** is to familiarize the students with the content of the chapter before reading, which will aid in their comprehension. These activities should be reviewed aloud prior to reading the chapter. Many of the Pre-reading activities were written for oral discussion but some can be easily adapted to paper-and-pencil activities.

The **Comprehension Questions** should be reviewed aloud prior to reading the chapter to further increase the student's comprehension, though obviously most of them can only be answered after reading.

I use a variety of techniques for reading the chapters: I read some of the chapters aloud, the students volunteer and take turns reading aloud, several capable readers divide the chapter and read aloud, or the students read silently. My experience has identified no dominant student preference among these approaches. The technique you select for reading should be based on the reading ability and comprehension skills of your students.

The Comprehension Questions were written to accommodate varying student abilities and in consideration of classroom time. After reading the chapter, some of the questions/activities may be discussed aloud or written. When time is an issue, I assign a particular question or two to each student for oral discussion. We may also complete some of the paper-and-pencil activities.

The final section of each chapter's activities is the **Post-reading Activities**. Many of these activities encourage hands-on creativity through coloring and drawing. Research skills and the presentation of oral reports are also emphasized in this section. Completion of these activities should be dictated by student interest and the availability of classroom time.

There are no tests or quizzes included in the lesson plans. Your creation of these activities will be based upon the needs of your students.

The **Resources** listed at the end of the manual are excellent sources of information to expand your teaching of Florida history and ecology using *A Land Remembered*. Many of them will be referred to throughout the manual.

Some Housekeeping Ideas

1. I suggest the following to ensure the security of the books and to discourage damage. Use a nonwashable marker to number each of the books. Mark two-pronged folders with numbers corresponding to the numbered books. For example, book number one will be kept with folder number one. Assign each student a numbered book and folder. You will be able to keep track of the classroom set of books and folders using this numbering and student assignment method. Repeat this process prior to beginning Volume Two.

2. Place copies of the lesson plans in the student's numbered folder as you begin each chapter. Students who are absent should be instructed to refer to the folder for lessons/activities completed during their absence.

Teacher Introduction to *A Land Remembered*

1. Discuss the reasoning and challenges of people throughout history who have chosen to resettle.

2. Solicit real life experiences of resettlement from the students.

3. Examine and discuss a map of Florida from 1858 when the main characters migrated to Florida from Georgia.

4. Briefly discuss a timeline of major historical events in the United States from 1776 to the present. Focus on the events from 1858–1880.

5. Briefly discuss a timeline of major historical events which occurred in Florida from 1858–1880. Use *Florida Portrait* for picture references for the major historical events. The students may create a timeline of events in Florida's history from your discussion.

6. Discuss the map of Florida from the novel as it pinpoints the locations and dates of important events in the lives of the main characters. The students will be directed to refer back to the map in the front of the book as they read Volumes One and Two.

7. Have the students use a current map of Florida to locate present-day cities/landmarks which are located in the same area as the dated locations on the map in the novel.

8. Examine pictures of people who lived in Florida in the mid-1800s. Include pictures of their homes, towns, farms, jobs, modes of transportation, and the physical environment of Florida. Use the pictures to encourage the students to draw conclusions about the people's way of life and the impact of living in harsh environments as compared to living in towns. Discuss the lack of educational opportunities. Resources: *Priceless Florida, The Young Naturalist's Guide to Florida, Florida's Fabulous Natural Places, Atlas of Florida,* and *Florida Portrait.*

9. Introduce the names of the main characters.

10. Read page 1 aloud. Discuss why the characters in the book use nonstandard English and discuss regional dialects within the United States.

11. Each time a chapter is dated, such as the date 1863 (Chapter 1, page 1) and 1866 (Chapter 7, page 46), instruct the students to refer to the map at the front of the book. Point out that the story location or time may change when a paragraph begins with a large capital letter, e.g., pages 3 and 6.

Volume 1 1863–1880
Chapter 1

Vocabulary/Slang

brogan, fetch, shinny up a tree, gut shoot, entrails, tote, oxen, adz, crosscut saw, auger bit, froe, drawing knife, homestead, lean-to, predators, robust, sharecropper, lard, scald the hog, cracklins, boiled pokeweed, flat bread, vittles, pone of cornbread, swamp cabbage, hanker, varmints, coon

Pre-reading Activities

1. See the map in the front of the book to pinpoint the location dated 1858.

2. What necessities would you pack if your family had to migrate to another state?

3. In the *Atlas of Florida* or *Priceless Florida* locate pictures and pertinent data that describe the Florida Scrub and High Pine and Temperate Hardwood Forest/Hammock habitats.

4. What conclusions can you draw about the physical environment of the MacIvey homestead from your research?

5. Read from *Florida's Past, Volume 2,* "The Pioneers of Opportunity" page 49.

Comprehension Questions

1. Fold a piece of notebook paper lengthwise into three columns. Label each column with the name of one of the main characters. List the physical and personality characteristics for Tobias, Zech, and Emma MacIvey in their column.

2. List the necessities Tobias and Emma bring with them when they migrate from Georgia to Florida.

3. List the household/food items described on page 5, paragraph 5. Next to each household item write the name of a similar item used today. For example:
    coal oil lamp — electric lights

4. List the animals in this chapter. Write the word *predator* next to the animals that the MacIveys fear. Write the word *helpful* next to the animals that provide help to the family.

5. List the food consumed by the MacIveys. Place a check mark next to any of these food products you have eaten.

Post-reading Activities

1. Complete/discuss teacher-selected Comprehension Questions.

2. Begin a family tree of the MacIvey family.

3. Make a family tree of your family members. Share any old family trees which go back many generations.

4. Sample fried pork rinds, which are the modern-day version of cracklins.

5. Sample canned hearts of palm. For information on swamp cabbage, see *Florida's Fabulous Trees* or *The Trees of Florida* and *My Florida.*

6. Draw a Florida Scrub and High Pine habitat. Include plants, animals, land forms, water sources. Resource: *Priceless Florida.* Also draw the negative impact humans have had on the ecosystem.

7. Draw a Temperate Hardwood Forest/Hammock. Include plants, animals, land forms, water sources. Resource: *Priceless Florida.* Discuss the impact humans have had on the ecosystem.

Chapter 2

Vocabulary/Slang

tattered, curs, muskets, private property, rustling, et, ravenously, marrow, marshtackie

Pre-reading Activities

1. In the *Atlas of Florida* or *Priceless Florida* locate pictures and pertinent data that describe a Florida Swamp habitat. You will learn that a swamp is actually a forested wetland and that the other types of wetlands are bogs and marshes. For information on the cypress tree see *Florida's Fabulous Trees* or *The Trees of Florida* and *The Young Naturalist's Guide to Florida.*

2. Research to find maps which pinpoint the location of the present-day Seminole reservations in Florida and Oklahoma. The location of reservations in Florida are found in a map in *Patchwork: Seminole and Miccosukee Art and Activities.*

3. Read the section from *Lament of the Cracker Cowboy* that describes the Seminole Indian cowboys.

Comprehension Questions

1. Who are Keith Tiger, Bird Jumper, and Lillie running from?

2. Why does Keith Tiger believe it is acceptable to kill and eat a cow with "no marking on it"?

3. Why are the Seminoles running away?

4. How does Tobias help the Seminoles?

5. In consideration of his treatment of the Seminoles, what conclusions can you draw about Tobias's character?

6. Describe the marshtackie.

7. How did the Seminoles once use the marshtackie?

8. Why do the Seminoles leave before dawn?

Post-reading Activities

1. Complete/discuss teacher-selected Comprehension Questions.

2. Research and report to the class the early history of the Seminoles as they migrated from Georgia and Alabama to north and central Florida. Include timelines and be able to pinpoint their migration route on a map of the southeastern United States. From *The Florida Reader,* "Indians and Blacks" pages 81–83, read an excellent description of the Seminole migration into Florida and their identification with and acceptance of runaway slaves.

3. Research and report to the class the Seminole Indian Wars with the United States. Include timelines and be able to pinpoint the location of important events and battles. The book *Hunted Like a Wolf* was written for young people and chronicles the Second Seminole War. It describes how the Seminoles and their allies effectively resisted an army ten times their size and frustrated the efforts of six generals.

4. Research and report to the class the current status of the Seminole Indians living in Florida and Oklahoma.

5. Research and report to the class the unique characteristics of Seminole culture. Include visuals in your presentation. The book *Patchwork* is an excellent reference in its description of Seminole culture. It also teaches students how to make Seminole patchwork designs with colored paper.

6. Research and report on some aspect of the history of the Florida Seminoles. Here are ideas from *Florida's Past*. In *Volume 1* read the following stories which are pertinent to Seminole history: *"Osceola: The Seminole Patriot," "Bartram Remembers Florida's Eden,"* and *"The Dogs of War Who Were Puppies."* In *Volume 2* read "The Seminoles' Friendliest Foe," and in *Volume 3* read *"The Tragedy of a Native Pocahontas,"* "Of Red Hopes and White Politics," "The Indians Last Warpath: Billy Bowlegs," and "Massacre in Southeast Florida."

7. Research the history, design, and significance of cattle brands.

8. Design your own personal cattle brand. Display the brands in the classroom.

9. Draw a Florida Swamp habitat. Include plants, animals, land forms, and water sources. Also draw the negative impact of human interference in the ecosystem. *Priceless Florida* is an excellent resource.

Chapter 3

Vocabulary/Slang

scrub, muscadine vines, Spanish moss, palmetto frond, skeeters, Reb soldiers, Federal troops, tallow, mite, hankering, afore, sanctuary, quilting bee, boar

Pre-reading Activities

1. Refer to the *Atlas of Florida* or *Priceless Florida* to locate pictures and pertinent data that describe a Florida freshwater marsh.

2. Locate pictures of an egret, heron, and wood ibis. Describe any sightings of these birds.

4. Use a map of Florida to locate the following: St. Johns River, Jacksonville, St. Andrews Bay on the Gulf of Mexico, Palatka, Gainesville.

5. Use a map of the southeastern United States to locate the city of Savannah, Georgia.

6. Use a map of the Caribbean to locate the country of Cuba.

7. Use a map showing the United States of America and the Confederate States of America to describe the social and economic differences between the two regions.

Comprehension Questions

1. Describe how the Civil War is affecting the following locations described on pages 16 and 17: Jacksonville, Florida; Savannah, Georgia; Cuba; St. Andrews Bay on the Gulf of Mexico; Palatka, Florida; Gainesville, Florida.

2. What deprivations are the Confederate soldiers suffering?

3. Why are Florida's cattle needed by the Confederate soldiers?

4. What is the job of the Rebel Cow Cavalry?

5. List the four problems/dangers created by the Civil War which affect the scrub "sanctuary" of the MacIveys.

6. What two fears does Emma express to Tobias?

7. What are her unspoken "yearnings"?

8. What two requests does Zech make to Tobias?

9. Which request is rejected?

Post-reading Activities

1. Complete/discuss teacher-selected Comprehension Questions.

2. Draw the trading post and setting as described on page 15.

3. Draw and accurately color pictures of an egret, heron, and wood ibis. See *Florida's Birds*.

4. Draw a Florida freshwater marsh. Include plants, animals, land forms, water sources. See chapter 10 in *Priceless Florida*. Also draw the negative impact humans have had on the ecosystem.

Chapter 4

Vocabulary/Slang

foliage, yonder, canebrake, yellowhammer, relished, varmints

Pre-reading Activities

1. Refer to the *Atlas of Florida* and *Priceless Florida* to locate pictures and pertinent data which describe a pine flatwoods habitat.

2. Locate a picture of a Carolina parakeet.

3. Locate a picture of an Andalusian bull, the breed which originated in Andalusia, Spain, and was first brought to Florida by Juan Ponce de León.

4. Why did Florida's early settlers have to preserve meat?

5. Research the methods of preserving meat by smoking and salting.

Comprehension Questions

1. How do rattlesnakes warn an intruder?

2. Describe the Carolina parakeet.

3. What negative factors affected the Carolina parakeet population and caused their extinction?

4. What unusual habit of the Carolina parakeet does Tobias describe to Zech?

5. Why is the deer manure important to the hunters?

6. Describe the wild cattle Tobias has seen in the woods.

7. List the five ways the bull parts are used.

Post-reading Activities

1. Complete/discuss teacher-selected Comprehension Questions.

2. Draw a pine flatwoods habitat. Include plants, animals, land forms, water sources. Also draw the negative impact humans have had on the ecosystem.

Chapter 5

Vocabulary/Slang

collards, able-bodied, savanna, smokehouse, shotgun, scrounged, ruckus

Pre-reading Activities

1. Trace the route of the cattle drive from Florida's Alachua savanna to the St. Marys River where soldiers will herd them up to Atlanta, Georgia.

2. Research to locate a picture and description of the McClellan military saddle which became popular with Florida cowcatchers after the Civil War.

3. The wild Florida cattle were left from the Spanish explorations and abandoned Spanish cattle ranches. According to *A Florida Cattle Ranch,* the first Florida cowmen preferred the title cowcatcher to cowboy. Early Florida cowcatchers did not chase and rope wild cattle because the cattle hid in the dense vegetation and had to be rooted out into the open using dogs. The Florida cowcatcher would then wrestle the cows to the ground, tie up the cows' legs, and brand them. The cows would be released to roam and feed until it was time for the Florida cowboy to round them up and drive them to market to be sold. Why was the McClellan military saddle better suited to catching the wild Florida cows as compared to the horned saddle used by Western cowboys?

4. Read from page 214, paragraph 3 to page 215, paragraph 3 in *The Florida Reader* for a description of the origin of the term *cracker,* which refers to early and native Floridians.

Comprehension Questions

1. What is the state marshal, Henry Addler, commissioned to do by the governor of the state of Florida?

2. Why is the patrol Tobias was forced to join called the Cow Cavalry?

3. Why is illiteracy not a handicap or embarrassment to Tobias?

4. What American nation are the states of Florida and Georgia part of?

5. Why do Emma's reactions on page 28, paragraph 11 and page 29, paragraph 9 indicate that she is a brave, unselfish woman?

6. The new recruits of the Cow Cavalry are provided with what three necessary items?

7. Why does a McClellan military saddle not have a horn like a cowboy saddle?

8. How are the wild swamp cattle that the Cow Cavalry must herd and drive different from Western cattle?

9. If you had no choice, would you give a thief the contents of your refrigerator or the family automobiles? Does Zech make the same choice as you?

10. How many gold one-dollar coins does Tobias receive at the end of the drive?

11. Why was gold more valuable than paper money?

12. What item does the state marshal allow Tobias to keep?

13. What natural ability does Zech have as a child that Henry Addler has as an adult?

Post-reading Activities

1. Complete/discuss teacher-selected Comprehension Questions.

2. In the form of a cartoon with multiple, sequential scenes, draw the description on page 32, paragraphs 1 and 2, of Zech defending his mother.

Chapter 6

Vocabulary/Slang

martial* law, cavalry, foot soldier, yonder, whupped, scabbard, ravenously, Confederate deserters

*Please note that some copies of the book have the incorrect spelling "marshal" and later printings have the correct spelling "martial." Discuss the difference in meaning and how this mistake could have been made.

Pre-reading Activities

1. Using a map of the United States of America, trace the route of the Federal troops from Hilton Head, South Carolina, to the mouth of the St. Johns River and south to Olustee, which is a few miles east of Lake City, Florida.

2. From *Florida's Past, Volume 1* read *"A Private's Eye-View of the Olustee Battle"* and *"Governor Milton: A Civil War Tragedy,"* and from *Volume 3, "*Native Rebs Against the Rebels.*"

3. On a map of Florida, locate the cities of Baldwin, Gainesville, Tallahassee, and Jacksonville.

Comprehension Questions

1. The whip is providing the family with what meat?

2. What is the second job Tobias is recruited to do in support of the Confederate army?

3. List the names of the Florida cities the Federal/Union troops have raided.

4. Why are the Northern soldiers taking black people in their raids?

5. Why is the color of a soldier's uniform important in battle? "Tobias wondered what would have happened if they were all dressed in overalls as he was." What do you think would have happened if the soldiers had been dressed like Tobias?

6. What valuable items does Tobias take from the dead soldier? How does the number of items identify the soldier as a Federal?

7. Why is it important to Tobias to say to the soldier, "I ain't stealing from the dead"?

8. How would your opinion of Tobias have changed if he had taken personal items from the soldier, such as a locket?

9. Why is Tobias so angry about the destruction of the house, smokehouse, barn, and the theft of the ox?

10. Why do you think Tobias told Zech he got the horse "off a dead soldier. A Federal"?

11. Why does Tobias decide to move the family further south?

Post-reading Activities

1. Complete/discuss teacher-selected Comprehension Questions.

2. Research and report on the Battle of Olustee.

3. Research to find how Florida's girls and women coped with the deprivations they suffered during the Civil War. For example, when there was no cobbler to make her shoes, a once-wealthy young girl made shoes out of corn shucks lined with velvet.

Chapter 7

Vocabulary/Slang

pallet (for sleeping), impenetrable, chickees, passel, Dutch oven

Pre-reading Activities

1. On the map in the front of the book, locate the Kissimmee River 1864.

2. Pinpoint the location of the Kissimmee River on a new map of Florida.

Comprehension Questions

1. What is the problem with trying to use a cavalry-trained horse to catch cows in the wild?

2. Why does Tobias stand for an hour looking at the MCI brand on the cow?

3. What plants from the abandoned Seminole garden does Tobias use to begin his own garden?

4. What deprivations is Emma experiencing?

5. What childhood treats has Zech never experienced?

6. Considering that neither complain about what they don't have, describe Emma's and Zech's personalities.

7. What attitude does Emma have about their future when she tells Tobias, "There's nothing I need that can't wait"?

8. Why does Tobias consider Zech a "man-child"?

Post-reading Activities

1. Complete/discuss teacher-selected Comprehension Questions.

2. Draw a floor plan of the Kissimmee house as described on page 47 and a floor plan of your home as a comparison. See *Florida Heritage Education Program, A Series of Lesson Plans: Farm Life in the Early 1800s*, and *Classic Cracker: Florida's Wood-Frame Vernacular Architecture*.

3. Use a map to find what town or city is 50 miles east of where you live. Imagine having to ride by horseback to this location to buy groceries!

4. Research to locate a picture of a Seminole Chickee. (Look on the website for the Florida State Archives photographic collection at www.floridamemory.com.)

5. Research to locate a picture of a Dutch oven and a description of how to cook in a Dutch oven.

6. Use the Internet to find a Dutch oven recipe for cooking beans. Get permission from school administration to cook the beans outside in a Dutch oven. A charcoal grill would work if an open fire is not allowed.

7. For classroom viewing, ask your school media specialist to purchase the film *The Yearling,* starring Gregory Peck and Jane Wyman. This is an excellent film that depicts the life of a family living in rural Florida in the late 1800s. It is based on the story by Marjorie Kinnan Rawlings.

Chapter 8

Vocabulary/Slang

savanna, proprietor, schooner, polecat, drifters, buckboard, sofkee

Pre-reading Activities

1. Find pictures and a description of a Florida prairie in *The Young Naturalist's Guide to Florida* or *Priceless Florida.*

2. Locate pictures and descriptions of a cypress stand (also referred to as a cypress dome), cabbage palm, and a sago palm in *Florida's Fabulous Trees* or *The Trees of Florida.*

3. Pinpoint the location of Lake Okeechobee on a map of Florida.

4. From the Old Testament of the Bible, research to find information about the man named Ishmael.

Comprehension Questions

1. Why does the proprietor of the trading post want to trade in silver or gold coins and not Confederate money?

2. How has the Civil War affected people living in the South?

3. Who came upon Tobias when he stopped for the night on the return journey home from the trading post?

4. With whom have the Indians shared the story of the bravery of Tobias when he helped defend them from the Indian bounty hunters?

5. What are the names of Tobias's Indian friends?

6. Why won't the trading post owner sell guns or bullets to the Indians?

7. What items do Tobias and the Seminoles exchange?

8. As compared to the cavalry horse, what advantages does a marshtackie have for chasing cows in the swamp?

9. As explained by Keith Tiger to Tobias, describe the care of wild cattle.

10. What lifestyle change does Tobias realize he will have to make if he plans to own cattle?

11. What do the U. S. government soldiers call the Seminoles who wander with their herds?

12. Why do the soldiers call the Seminoles this name?

13. What three kindnesses are extended to Tobias by the Seminoles on page 59?

Post-reading Activities

1. Complete/discuss teacher-selected Comprehension Questions.

2. Research to find examples of Confederate bills.

Chapter 9

Vocabulary/Slang

flailing his arms, horse's flanks, bull cow, heifer cow, mite

Pre-reading Activity

Define the term *subsistence living*. How does the lifestyle of the MacIveys fit this term?

Comprehension Questions

1. Describe the marshtackie.

2. Describe the dogs.

3. Who left the horse and dogs for Tobias?

4. Why does Tobias name the marshtackie Ishmael?

5. What does Tobias name the dogs? (The meaning of the names from the 1800s is "equal in ability; even; neck and neck.")

6. Why don't the Seminoles wait to enjoy Tobias' reaction to their gifts?

7. Read the last paragraph on page 65. What feelings does Tobias share with Emma in this paragraph?

Post-reading Activities

1. Complete/discuss teacher-selected Comprehension Questions.

2. Draw Tobias riding the bull from the description on page 62.

Chapter 10

Vocabulary/Slang

mite, et, vittles, nigh, beholdin

Pre-reading Activity

Pinpoint the location of Tallahassee on a map of Florida.

Comprehension Questions

1. List the four cow-chasing and herding skills the dogs possess.

2. What two herding skills does Ishmael possess?

3. How do we know that the family is living in an isolated area where the land is not legally owned by Tobias or anyone else?

4. Describe the man who emerges from the palmetto clump.

5. What is he wearing?

6. What is the man's unusual name?

7. With what object do we usually associate the man's name?

8. Why did he leave his cabin and land?

9. What role will this man now have as part of the MacIvey Cattle Company?

10. What first relationship is Zech quickly developing with this new "family member"?

Post-reading Activities

1. Complete/discuss teacher-selected Comprehension Questions.

2. Use a map of Florida and the scale of miles to determine how many miles south the man has walked.

3. What would be your destination if you walked that far from the town in which you live?

4. Organize the class into sewing groups to cut from a pattern, mark, and sew, a simply designed pair of short pants similar to what Skillit wore. Have each group select a model to wear the short pants in a fashion show.

Chapter 11

Vocabulary/Slang

sommers, red cent, cracker sack*, britches, dressed meat, mite riled, sho'

*Look up "gunnysack" in the *American Heritage Dictionary* and you will find a note explaining the different names for this type of coarse material.

Pre-reading Activities

1. Research to find a picture and description of a stern-wheeler steamboat.

2. Use a map of Florida to pinpoint the location of the city of Okeechobee.

Comprehension Questions

1. What is Tobias' first business opportunity/plan to earn money from the many cows they have branded?

2. Why do Skillit's pants have no need for pockets?

3. What second business opportunity is provided from the needs expressed by the stern-wheeler captain?

4. Why do alligators cock their jaws open toward the sunlight?

5. List the seven attempts of the alligator to avoid being killed.

6. How much will the boat captain pay for an alligator hide?

7. Is the value of the hide worth the danger of trying to kill an alligator?

Post-reading Activity

Complete/discuss teacher-selected Comprehension Questions.

Chapter 12

Vocabulary/Slang

tarpaulin, skeeters, sommers, palm fronds, lean-to, lard, sultry, entrepreneur

Pre-reading Activities

1. Locate 1867 on the map in the front of the book. The map indicates that some of the cattle were drowned on a drive that is not described in the student version of the book. An indirect reference is made in Chapter 15, page 105.

2. Use a map of Florida to locate the cities of Jacksonville, Pensacola, and Key West.

3. Find the location of Punta Rassa on the map in the front of the book. Use a map of Florida to locate what present-day city is located near what was once Punta Rassa.

Comprehension Questions

1. What is the purpose of taking the cows from the swamp and beginning the first summer grazing drive?

2. What signal for trouble is to be used for whoever is out on watch?

3. What confidence does Tobias express regarding Emma's ability to adjust to "this wandering life"?

4. Why is Tobias willing to take his family and leave "the relative safety of his hidden hammock" for a cattle drive into unknown, unmapped territory?

5. What additional employees does Tobias realize he needs when he sees the profit potential of the large wild, untended herds?

6. What is Tobias's reaction to Zech's idea of fencing the land so they won't have to follow the cattle?

7. What new business opportunity does Tobias learn of in Fort Pierce?

8. How does Tobias's "vision" express business confidence in himself, Zech, and Skillit?

9. How much money will Tobias earn if he is able to get $12.00 for 148 cows?

10. What business decisions does Tobias make that reflect the thinking of an entrepreneur?

Post-reading Activities

1. Complete/discuss teacher-selected Comprehension Questions.

2. Tobias sees the Florida grazing land as worthless for farming and only good for feeding cows. How have various Florida landscapes been modified from their original design to fit human needs and demands? Include examples of habitat modification in your neighborhood that you have observed.

3. Research the introduction of citrus into Florida by the Spanish explorers and settlers.

4. Use the scale of miles on a map of Florida and the Caribbean to determine how far a journey the cattle will make from where they are sold at Punta Rassa to Havana, Cuba.

5. Use a map of Florida to trace the directions to Punta Rassa given by the store owner to Tobias on page 8, paragraph 7.

6. Use a map of Florida to determine what northern, western, eastern, and southern cities we have located so far in our reading and study of *A Land Remembered*.

7. Find a picture of a wood-burning stove and a description of how this non-electric stove cooked and baked food.

8. Go to the Bureau of Labor Statistics website http://stats.bls.gov/ to find how the Consumer Price Index has been calculated to show the change in how much a dollar can buy from year to year.

9. Invite an entrepreneur to speak with the class regarding the sacrifices and rewards of entrepreneurship.

Chapter 13

Vocabulary/Slang

liable, tarpaulin, yonder, unabated

Pre-reading Activities

1. **What ocean is Tobias speaking of when he tells Skillit, "Must be a storm coming from out over the ocean"?**

2. Why were the animals running rapidly westward?

Comprehension Questions

1. Why is the marsh a dangerous location during the storm?

2. What area provides safety for the family and animals?

3. What is the most valuable thing lost in the storm? How does Tobias react to the loss? What does his reaction imply about his ability to recover from misfortune and his role as a leader/entrepreneur?

Post-reading Activities

1. Complete/discuss teacher-selected Comprehension Questions.

2. Draw the flooded area as described on page 93, paragraphs 2 and 3.

Chapter 14

Vocabulary/Slang

corral, to get calves mammied-up, venison, drovers, sparse, clapboard buildings, residential section of town, sauntered, dismounting, dejectedly, Tobias will pay "Fifty cents a day plus keep" (define *keep* in this context), betwix, double take, innards, afore, unison, gaunt, purty

Pre-reading Activities

1. Pinpoint the date 1868 on the map in the front of the book. Where is the setting for this date?

2. Locate Punta Rassa on the same map. On what body of water is Punta Rassa located?

3. Research the history of the town of Punta Rassa, Florida.

4. See *Florida Portrait* page 111 for a picture of a stern-wheeler like the Osceola to which Zech and Skillit sold venison and raccoon hides.

Comprehension Questions

1. What plan to expand their number of employees do Emma and Tobias develop?

2. What is Emma's response to Tobias's lack of confidence?

3. Read page 98, paragraph 5. With what in today's fast-food restaurants does the "window cut into the side of the building" compare?

4. How long has it been since the man Tobias offers a job as cattle herder/driver "went down to a creek and washed"?

5. Why do you think hiring Frog and Bonzo has motivated Tobias to have the sign "MacIvey Cattle Company" made?

Post-reading Activities

1. Complete/discuss teacher-selected Comprehension Questions.

2. Define the term *entrepreneur*. Describe what kind of business you would like to own if you have considered becoming a future entrepreneur.

Chapter 15

Vocabulary/Slang

ferry, passel, pine knot*, cypress knees, slough, muck, vittles, stagnant, apparition

*The area on a pine tree where a branch grows. Knots were cut from felled pine trees. Due to the concentration of sap where the branch grows from the tree, the knots are very hard and flammable. (Special thanks to old-time Cracker Thom Nix for the explanation of pine knots.)

Pre-reading Activities

1. Locate the Kissimmee River on a map of Florida.

2. See *Florida's Fabulous Trees* or *The Trees of Florida* for pictures and descriptions of a cypress hammock/dome, cypress knees, and the bald cypress tree.

3. Read the *Atlas of Florida*, pages 80, 81, and 101, and *Florida Portrait*, pages 100, 105, 106, and 123, for information on open-range ranching and the cracker cowboys. Also see *A Florida Cattle Ranch*.

4. Read one of the Cracker Westerns to learn more about Florida cowboys (and they're fun to read).

Comprehension Questions

1. What does it mean to "give someone your word"?

2. How do Tobias and Sam Lowery informally execute their business agreement? Why is this type of agreement not used in business transactions today?

3. What new business idea does Tobias consider "worth thinking on"?

4. On page 111 Emma says, "I've never heard so many different sounds at one time." List the seven chilling sounds Emma hears as described on pages 108 and 109.

5. What worrisome feelings do Frog, Skillit, and Zech express as they move the herd further into the narrow swamp?

6. How does the fire at the wagon give them a sense of direction in the dark of night?

7. What neighborhood landmarks give you direction?

8. What is the difference between milk cows and the cows the MacIvey Cattle Company is herding?

9. Why would the owner of a milk cow "bell the cow"?

10. What do you think is making the tinkling bell sound?

11. What ecosystem is described on page 116, paragraph 2?

12. Identify and describe the man who wore the bells?

13. Why didn't Tobias tell Zech the source of the tinkling bells?

14. What did the six cows do when they "reached the point where water met solid ground"?

15. If some of the cattle he entrusted to Tobias to sell don't make it to Punta Rassa, how does Tobias guarantee Windell Lykes payment?

16. Why is this guarantee a smart business decision for Tobias?

17. Why is Tobias nervous and unable to sleep the night before they reach Punta Rassa?

18. How is Tobias' drive to succeed different from his father's?

19. How has Tobias proved himself a positive role model for Zech?

Post-reading Activities

1. Complete/discuss teacher-selected Comprehension Questions.

2. Research and report to the class: the location of settlements of the native Florida Indian tribe the Timucua, the unusual characteristics of their culture, and their destruction at the hands of European explorers.

3. Describe a personal incident or story in which an animal has sensed danger and given a warning.

4. Describe any personal alligator encounters.

5. Why are alligators no longer on the endangered species list? See the *Atlas of Florida* for information on alligator hunting.

6. What are the risks in owning and operating your own business?

7. Color the picture of the cracker cowboy found in the coloring book *They Called It Florida.*

Chapter 16

Vocabulary/Slang

livery stable, blacksmith shop, adjacent, side-wheel steamboat (as compared to a stern-wheeler), desolate, ledgers, chambray shirt, Spanish gold doubloon, steamer trunk, flaunt, door stoop, sto-bought, bandanna, sucker bet, calliope, racial discrimination, prejudice, integration

Pre-reading Activities

1. What is the meaning of the saying "owners of dairy farms and cattle ranches smell the money and not the manure"?

2. Locate a picture of a steamer trunk. Why did travelers in the late 1800s need such a large trunk?

3. Bring in a chambray shirt to show the class.

4. Locate a picture of a calliope.

Comprehension Questions

1. From what country did the rum originate?

2. Why is Cap'n Hendry going to pay Tobias the higher dollar amount for each cow in the herd?

3. How much more is Tobias going to be paid for each cow than the amount he was quoted in Chapter 12?

4. Why is Tobias paid in Spanish gold doubloons?

5. Why is the money safe from thieves in Punta Rassa?

6. Why does the waiter discriminate against Skillit?

7. The integration of restaurants began with the Civil Rights legislation of the 1960s. Use the date 1960 to determine how many years have passed between the discrimination of Skillit in the cafe and the passage of laws forbidding discrimination due to race.

8. How do Tobias and Frog react to the discrimination against Skillit?

9. What is Tobias threatening when he tells the waiter that the owner of the cafe is "going to have some real bad trouble with the roof next time it rains"?

10. What does Frog mean when he says, "That much money will probably burn a hole in my pockets"?

11. What memories will the first coin earned by the MacIvey Cattle Company always hold for Zech?

12. What does Skillit mean when he describes his new outfit as the "first sto-bought stuff I ever owned"?

13. How does Emma react when she is told that no women's dresses are available? What does her reaction reveal about her character?

14. How will Emma's surprise gift make her life easier?

15. What does Frog know about Ishmael that causes him to bet against Hendry's horse, Thunder, in a 3-mile race?

16. Frog wagers $200 in a five-to-one bet that Ishmael will win the race. How much will he win if Ishmael beats Thunder?

17. What does Tobias win with Ishmael's victory?

18. What prediction does Mr. Hendry make about Zech's future?

19. What does Frog mean when he says, "I just got four years' pay for nothing"?

20. Why does Tobias refuse a drink of the rum?

21. Why do you think Skillit is looking for "colored folk" in Punta Rassa?

22. Why does the ferry tender think the wagon and its contents and the appearance of the members of the cattle company look like they belong to a circus?

Post-reading Activities

1. Complete/discuss teacher-selected Comprehension Questions.

2. What sound business decisions and sacrifices have Tobias and Emma made that result in this first financial success?

3. Why do business owners sometimes frame and display the first dollar they've earned?

4. Share incidents in which you, a family member, or someone you know, was discriminated against because of his/her race, sex, age, or ethnic background.

5. When Frog speaks of the café owner serving a black man for the first time, he says, "He just learned that some things you do for the first time ain't nearly as bad as you thought it'd be." Share first-time experiences that caused you unnecessary worry.

6. Draw a picture of Skillit in his new outfit or draw and cut his outfit from colored construction paper and paste his outfit on a picture of Skillit.

7. Why does winning encourage a gambler to continue even though he loses more times than he wins?

8. To show his gratitude, how does Tobias reward Skillit, Bonzo, and Frog? Why is this an important personal and business decision?

9. Draw a picture of Emma's cook stove as described on page 136, paragraph 2.

Field Trip Idea

Make reservations at a local buffet which serves Southern country cooking. Sample turnip greens, black-eyed peas, corn bread, and other traditional Southern dishes.

Chapter 17

Vocabulary/Slang

palmetto thatch roof, cypress shingle roof, idle, cut (separate) the cattle, vittles, cows chewing their cuds, grub, hoe-down, frolic, fiddles, stay for a spell, cadence, punch to drink, lilac, sommers, bushwhackers, common grave, varmints, brogan shoes

Pre-reading Activities

1. Refer to the map of Florida in the book to determine the location of the MacIvey Cattle Company in 1875.

2. Describe a time when you were inside or outside in absolute darkness. Was there a campfire or light as a beacon to guide you?

3. Unlike people who lived in the 1800s, why are our eyes and senses unaccustomed to absolute darkness?

4. Refer to the map in the book to find the date and location of Fort Drum and the home of Glenda Turner.

5. Use a yardstick to see the length of a 40-inch gun barrel.

6. From *Florida's Past, Volume 1,* read *"Bone Mizell Was a Cowboy's Cowboy"* and from *Volume 3,* *"When Cowland Was Another Country,"* *"Jacob Summerlin: He Cracked His Whip Over An Empire,"* and *"The Stormy Reign of a Mighty Mite."*

Comprehension Questions

1. What does the additional steamer trunk indicate?

2. What tasty business venture are Tobias's cows eating away?

3. Why has their increased wealth not changed the lifestyle of the family?

4. How many years have passed since 1866 when Tobias and Zech caught their first cow in the swamp?

5. If he was six years old in 1863, how old is Zech now?

6. What "chore" do you think Skillit wants to accomplish with his request of additional time away from the hammock?

7. What "good idea" does Frog propose to Bonzo and Zech?

8. Why is Zech hesitant to go along with the "idea"?

9. What event causes Zech, Frog, and Bonzo to tarry instead of returning right away to the cows?

10. Describe Glenda Turner.

11. Why is Zech so uncomfortable at the frolic?

12. When does Zech promise to return to Fort Drum?

13. Why do the cabbage palms and palmetto look as though they "had turned to lilacs" to Zech?

14. What do Zech, Frog, and Bonzo discover when they return to the pen?

15. How can they tell that wild animals have not attacked the cows?

16. Why does Frog refer to the thieves as "bushwhackers"?

17. What angry vow does Zech make?

18. What is Tobias's reaction to the theft of the cows?

19. Who does Tobias believe was the original owner of the powerful gun used by the bushwhackers?

20. Why does the gun seem familiar to Zech?

21. What fatherly advice does Tobias give Zech about surviving in the wilderness?

22. What does Emma mean when she tells Zech, "I smelled like flowers once, but not anymore"? Does Emma seem angry that she "no longer smells like flowers"?

23. Besides a wagon full of orange trees, what does Skillit bring home?

24. What is Frog's attitude toward women and marriage when he says he doesn't want to "be tied to some woman's apron strings"?

Post-reading Activities

1. Complete/discuss teacher-selected Comprehension Questions.

2. Draw the MacIvey homestead as described on page 149, paragraph 6 with the addition of the cabins and barn near the garden area.

3. How is square dancing different from dances popular among young people today?

4. After dressing Bonzo's wound, Emma tells him to "go on and join that man talk." What is "man talk"?

5. Compare the "man talk" of Tobias, Zech, Frog, and Bonzo with "man talk" of today.

6. Give examples of how Tobias' advice on survival could be used by young people today who face challenging circumstances.

7. What positive and negative experiences in this chapter helped Zech grow from a boy to a man?

8. Compare Zech's experiences with the experiences of boys today which cause them to grow into men?

9. Why would a mother today not encourage her eighteen-year-old son to date a fourteen-year-old girl? Why is this acceptable in the 1800s?

10. Emma invites Pearlie Mae into the kitchen for "some woman talk." What is "woman talk"?

11. Compare the "woman/girl talk" of Emma and Pearlie Mae with "woman/girl talk" of today.

Chapter 18

Vocabulary/Slang

drought, horizon, vertical, horizontal, desecrated, molasses, lean-to, retched, pestilence

Pre-reading Activities

1. Why do animals and humans need salt in their diets?

2. Describe the life cycle of a mosquito.

3. Refer to the map in the book that indicates the date and location of where the mosquitoes killed the cows.

Comprehension Questions

1. Why is 30 acres required to feed just one cow?

2. Why is Tobias watching with concern the lightning strikes in the far west?

3. Describe the "retreat from natural instincts" that Zech witnesses as he watches the various animals share the pond of fresh drinking water?

4. Describe the "death cloud" that attacks the animals and humans.

5. Why is the "death cloud" as bad as a lightning strike on a dry prairie?

Post-reading Activities

1. Complete/discuss teacher-selected Comprehension Questions.

2. Make a lean-to of palmetto fronds in the classroom. If the use of real palmetto fronds is not possible, have the students draw, cut, and color palmetto fronds from butcher paper with which to construct the classroom lean-to.

3. Ask your school media specialist to order the videotape *Judge Platt: Tales of a Florida Cow-hunter*. This videotape is an excellent supplement to Volume 1.

Chapter 19

Vocabulary/Slang

Winchester repeating rifle, mite steep, reckon, betwix, vermin, up to snuff

Pre-reading Activities

1. Pinpoint the location of the Caloosahatchee River and Lake Okeechobee on a map of Florida.

2. Using a map of the states that border the Gulf of Mexico, locate the city of New Orleans, Louisiana. Trace the shipping route from New Orleans to the trading post on the Caloosahatchie River.

3. Locate a picture of a Winchester repeating rifle.

Comprehension Questions

1. When they were "at the MacIvey hammock once before," what did the Seminoles bring Tobias?

2. What circumstances have caused James Tiger and Willie Cypress to search for Tobias?

3. Describe the leopard dogs the Seminoles promise Zech as a replacement for Nip and Tuck.

4. For what reason has the American government denied the Seminoles the right to own cows?

5. Zech feels "deep sympathy" for those who suffer from hunger. What event is Zech referring to when he recalls that "even the animals were willing to share if it meant survival for all"?

6. How does the clerk justify the cost of the Winchester rifles to Tobias?

7. Who are the non-crew members for whom Tobias buys the additional rifles and bullets?

8. What does Tobias recognize in the cattle holding pen?

9. From whom did the man take the MacIvey cattle?

10. What is Tobias's reaction when he learns what the men had done to punish those who had his cattle?

11. Why does Tobias punish the men himself and not seek help from the law to settle the conflict?

12. Why does Tobias feel compelled to go to the Seminoles?

13. Why is Tobias confident he will meet with the Seminoles even though he does not know where their village is located?

14. What symptoms of illness has Bonzo experienced?

15. Why doesn't he go to the doctor for medicine?

Post-reading Activities

1. Complete/discuss teacher-selected Comprehension Questions.

2. What is Tobias saying to Zech when he tells him he must learn to handle the rifle like a man?

3. What does "take it like a man" mean? In what circumstances do males receive this advice? Is this advice valuable for males?

4. Which are "tougher," men or women?

5. During the late nineteenth century, exhibition and trick shooters at carnivals and rodeos created bullet art using Winchester rifles. These Winchester artists would shoot designs into tin targets. Students can create their own "bullet art" using black construction paper and a pointed object such as a pencil. Draw a simple sketch on a piece of black construction paper, and then puncture holes along the outline of the sketch, spacing them approximately half an inch apart. The "bullet art" should be displayed in a window, where the sunlight will shine through the holes, showing the designs.

Chapter 20

Vocabulary/Slang

dissuade, perplexed, rookeries, cane pole for fishing, sawgrass, impenetrable, air plants, dissipated, foliage, formidable, deerskin leggings, georgette, turban crowned with an egret plume, chickees, malaria, gourd bowl, sofkee, gruel, missionary, quinine, fret

Pre-reading Activities

1. On the map in the front of the book, locate Tobias's meeting with the Seminoles in 1875.

2. On a map of Florida locate the Caloosahatchee River and the 470,000-acre Lake Okeechobee. Follow this river as Tobias and Zech do on their journey southward from the lake and into the great swamp.

3. Using the maps and charts in the *Atlas of Florida* or the map in *Patchwork,* discuss the location and size of Seminole and Creek Indian reservations today.

4. Locate pictures of the great blue heron, snowy egret, white heron, wood ibis, whooping crane, anhinga, cormorants, coot, roseate spoonbills, limpkin, and everglades kite. (Many are found in the *Florida's Vanishing Wildlife Coloring Book* and *The Young Naturalist's Guide to Florida.* All are in *Florida's Birds.*) Draw or color and display pictures of these birds in your classroom.

5. Tobias and Zech ride through a dense custard-apple forest. Pond-apple trees belong to the custard-apple family. Pond-apple trees grow to be 40 to 50 feet tall and produce a flower with yellowish white petals an inch in diameter. The fruit of the tree is heart-shaped, 3 to 5 inches long, and light green in color. These trees grow only south of Pinellas County. How many times higher are pond-apple trees than the height of your classroom? Why don't these trees grow north of Pinellas County?

6. For an explanation and pictures of air plants, see *Florida's Fabulous Trees* and the *Young Naturalists Guide to Florida.* Bring samples into the classroom. (Spanish Moss should be treated for insects before bringing it in. You can do this by placing it in a microwave oven for fifteen to twenty seconds. Keep your eye on the moss while microwaving so it doesn't scorch.)

7. Zech and Tobias enter the great cypress swamp and see some cypress trees which are 70 feet in circumference at their base. Compare the circumference of the cypress with the circumference of your classroom. See *Florida Portrait* page 183 for a picture of a three-thousand-year-old cypress tree.

8. On a map of Florida locate the Ten Thousand Islands along the southern Gulf coast.

9. A friend offers to show Zech "the great marsh" described to him by James and Willie. The great marsh is also known by its Seminole Indian name, "Pay-Hay-Okee, the "River of Grass" or the grassy waters. Today the town of Pahokee is located near the Pahokee State Park on the southeastern shore of Lake Okeechobee in Palm Beach County. See the *Atlas of Florida* for a map of the Everglades and an explanation of "the river of grass." See *The Young Naturalist's Guide to Florida* for an excellent description of sawgrass and why the area was named for the unending sight of "ever" glades.

Comprehension Questions

1. What fear for the future of the Indian and the bounty of life found on the shores of Lake Okeechobee does Tobias express to Zech?

2. Moon flowers/vines are a tropical plant of the morning glory family. The vine produces a large, white, fragrant flower, that only blooms at night. Amazingly, what "first flight" is Zech able to make because of the density of the moon vines?

3. Does Willie's father seem to know the fate of his son?

4. What illness does Tobias have?

5. Bonzo has experienced the same symptoms as Tobias. From what did they contract this illness?

6. Describe Tawanda Cypress.

7. Why doesn't Tawanda sound like the other Seminoles when she speaks?

8. Rather than using paddles, why do Tawanda and Zech use thin poles to navigate the dugout cypress canoe?

9. In what two situations with Tawanda does Zech learn Seminole rules for a woman sitting with a man?

10. What "silent understanding" do Zech and Tawanda communicate?

11. What does Tobias need from the store in Fort Drum?

12. Who does Zech hope to see in the store?

13. Tobias is unashamed when he must admit that he cannot read and write. Why is Zech embarrassed to tell Glenda's father that he can't write her a letter?

14. When Tobias and Zech return home, who do they learn has not survived the attack of the death cloud?

15. Tobias describes the swamp as a "place so full of life." Count the number of animals mentioned from page 192, paragraph 2 to page 197, paragraph 1. (PLEASE do not mark in the book.)

Post-reading Activities

1. Complete/discuss teacher-selected Comprehension Questions.

2. Draw the custard-apple forest as described on page 194, paragraphs 1–5. Include the details and lush colors described by Zech.

3. Describe the clothing and adornments worn by Tony Cypress as described on page 197, paragraph 4. See *Florida Portrait* pages 73 and 87 for pictures of famous Seminole leaders.

4. How are the Seminole leaders' dress/adornments similar to that of Tony Cypress? See *Florida Portrait* page 186 for a picture of Seminoles dressed in their traditional clothing. *The Complete Book of Seminole Patchwork* is a good resource on the history of Seminole clothing and a how-to book on creating Seminole patchwork items. *Patchwork: Seminole and Miccosukee Art and Activities* is a book for students to learn how to do Florida Native American patchwork using colored construction paper.

5. Draw the Seminole village as described on page 199, paragraphs 1 and 2.

6. Find a picture of a Seminole chickee (there's one in *Patchwork*). Make a mini-chickee for the classroom from palm fronds or cut and color palm fronds from butcher paper.

7. Zech was given a gourd bowl of gruel called sofkee. Sofkee is ground corn which is boiled in water until the corn is very fine and soft. What favorite Southern breakfast food does this sound like? Bring in this breakfast food and prepare it in a crockpot for everyone to taste.

8. What does the roasted alligator taste like to Zech? Would you be willing to taste alligator meat? Describe the taste of alligator if you have eaten it. Request samples of alligator meat from a restaurant that offers this delicacy.

9. Keith Tiger tells Tobias and Zech to avoid the custard-apple forest upon their return home and to travel to the east side of Lake Okeechobee, near the ocean. What ocean is he referring to?

10. Create a classroom Seminole patchwork sampler as shown in *Patchwork*.

11. A fun classroom activity is student creation of individual quilt squares. Solicit the help of parent volunteers who are familiar with quilting. Provide each student with a one-gallon plastic bag labeled with his or her name and class period. The plastic

bags for each class period should be kept in separate boxes. In each bag place a six-inch square of batting, two six-inch squares of fabric, an eight-inch piece of yarn, and a needle. A classroom sewing supply table should contain various colors of thread, quilting pins, colored pencils for marking, and scissors. Your parent volunteers can demonstrate how to sew the batting to the squares and how to turn the square right side out. Parent volunteers can demonstrate simple quilt stitching designs. The students can also sew buttons, beads, and sequins on the quilt squares to further personalize them. The yarn is sewn to the top two corners of the square for hanging the square for display. School visitors enjoyed my students' individual quilt squares, which were displayed in our main office.

Chapter 21

Vocabulary/Slang

canter, bolt of cloth, clan, pot-bellied stove

Pre-reading Activities

1. What is the best gift you have ever given?

2. What is the best gift you have ever received?

3. Ask someone seventy years old or older to describe the best gifts he/she received as a child. Report your findings to the class.

4. Describe a situation in which you felt out of place.

Comprehension Questions

1. Why have the MacIveys never celebrated Christmas in a festive way with a tree, by exchanging wrapped gifts, with dancing, or attending a church service?

2. With their increased income, Tobias now purchases store-bought gifts. What will Emma do with a bolt of cloth?

3. Describe the differences between Glenda and Tawanda.

4. Which one would be the best wife for Zech? Explain your answer.

5. Why is Glenda's father impressed with Zech when he purchases apples for Ishmael and how do we know that he likes Zech?

6. Why is it important that Mr. Turner like Zech?

7. Why does Zech feel anger toward his parents and then shame for his angry feelings?

8. Why didn't Zech notice the moth holes, torn seams, frayed collars and cuffs, missing buttons, and too-short sleeves and pants on the clothes of the other men and boys?

9   Is Glenda giving Zech accurate advice when she tries to make him feel better by comparing his first clumsy attempt to dance with his first attempt to ride Ishmael?

10. Describe Glenda's behavior toward Zech which indicates that she is not shy in expressing her feelings for him.

11. What do Glenda and her parents know about her and Zech that he does not?

12. Is Zech clumsy and hesitant to kiss Glenda?

13. Why does Zech need to be alone to think about his relationship with Glenda?

14. Why is Tawanda able to make Zech feel at ease while Glenda makes him feel shy?

15. Why can't Zech see himself through Glenda's eyes?

16. What does Emma mean when she tells Zech, "Girls want a man, not some fancy dancer who couldn't skin a rabbit if his family was starving"?

17. What advice would you have given Zech to help him cope with his insecure feelings?

Post-reading Activities

1. Complete/discuss teacher-selected Comprehension Questions.

2. What characteristics do women look for when choosing the man they want to marry?

3. What characteristics do men look for when choosing the woman they want to marry?

4. Divide a piece of paper in half lengthwise. List the people who have been Zech's "teachers" on the left side of the paper. List Zech's positive and negative characteristics on the right side of the paper. Draw lines to connect the "teacher" to the characteristic he or she has helped Zech develop.

5. List the people who have been the most influential "teachers" in your life. What positive and negative characteristics have they helped you develop?

6. Draw a picture of Glenda or cut out a picture in a magazine of someone who you feel looks as Glenda is described.

Chapter 22

Vocabulary/Slang

cow fodder, acre, deed, squatters, mercantile store, blunderbuss, ain't joshin', much obliged, purtiest, dainty

Pre-reading Activities

1. Describe how orange blossoms smell. How does the smell of real orange blossoms compare with the smell of orange blossom perfume?

2. Taste orange blossom honey on crackers. How does orange blossom honey compare with honey made from the nectar of other flowers?

3. See *Florida Portrait* pages 216 and 217, for pictures and information regarding the state-mandated end of open-range grazing in 1951.

4. See *Florida Portrait* page 129 for a picture of a typical central Florida town similar to one Zech would have visited in the 1880s.

5. What is the purpose of having a title/deed to property?

Comprehension Questions

1. What new business does Tobias see as their future?

2. Why is this new venture easier than the cattle business?

3. What does Tobias see when he compares a whole herd of cows with all the blooms on the trees?

4. For what upcoming event is Emma sewing a dress?

5. What is worrying Zech about Tobias's orange grove?

6. How has the cattle business changed since Tobias and Zech first caught cows in the wild?

7. What now threatens open-range grazing of cattle?

8. Why doesn't Tobias think he needs to buy the land on which they live and graze their cattle?

9. What catches Zech's eye as he is leaving town?

10. Describe your feelings as Zech, without the help of Frog and Skillit, approaches the camp of the men who had sold his father's gun.

11. Zech finds an "empty gallon jug with a corn cob stopper." What did this jug once contain?

12. What vow does Zech make after kicking the jug into the creek?

13. How many acres does Zech buy?

14. How much gold did he spend at 20 cents an acre?

15. Why is Zech confused by the way Emma expresses her thanks for the store-bought dress?

Post-reading Activities

1. Complete/discuss teacher-selected Comprehension Questions.

2. See *Florida Portrait* page 124 for an interesting account of the feud between the Barber and Mizell cattle families. Creative writers can write a play from the account to be performed in the classroom.

3. Local government can legally take property from the owner if the property taxes are not paid. The property is then sold to recoup the loss of tax dollars. Check the classified section of the newspaper to compare how much Zech pays for an acre of land as compared to the cost of acreage in Florida today. How does the cost of prime acreage compare with less desirable land?

4. Watch the thirty-minute videotape *Citrus Farming for Kids*.

5. Watch the videotape *The Honey Files*.

Chapter 23

Vocabulary/Slang

hang like a hawg at scrapin' time, purty, joshing, lawsy me, sho', fittin', schooner, fust, youngens, blister yo' hiney, itinerant preacher

Pre-reading Activity

Use a map of Florida to trace the honeymoon journey of Glenda and Zech from Fort Drum to Fort Pierce, where they boarded an inland schooner which sailed from Fort Pierce to Jacksonville and returned to Fort Pierce.

Comprehension Questions

1. Why are the suits making Zech and Tobias itch?

2. What do the white flowers on the door of the store indicate?

3. Describe the wedding ring Zech gives Glenda.

4. What special doubloon could the ring be made from?

Post-reading Activities

1. Complete/discuss teacher-selected Comprehension Questions.

2. Add Glenda MacIvey's name to the MacIvey family tree.

Volume 2   1880–1968
Chapter 24

Vocabulary/Slang

carcass, gaunt, singeing, knickknacks, "let's quit the jawin' "

Pre-reading Activity

Examine the dates and locations on the map of Florida in the front of the book. Concentrating on the dates between 1875 and 1968, discuss the differences between how the twentieth century is dated and how the nineteenth century is dated, as well as the names of new characters, and how the settings for Volume 2 are primarily located in south Florida.

Comprehension Questions

1. Which organs are the thieves removing from the carcasses of the cattle?

2. Do you agree with Skillit's reasoning for the killing and waste of the cow meat?

3. Why does Glenda, and not Emma, have the ability to open "a previously unknown world" to Zech?

4. What new knowledge does Emma believe books, music, and church services can give the new Zech MacIvey family?

5. What value does Glenda see in being Zech's "partner" as well as his wife?

6. What secret does Glenda share with Emma?

Post-reading Activities

1. Complete/discuss teacher-selected Comprehension Questions.

2. What can husbands and wives do to make their spouses happy?

Chapter 25

Vocabulary/Slang

torn asunder, low (in reference to cattle), buckboard

Pre-reading Activities

1. Locate a picture of a buckboard.

2. What do we now know about the dangers of excessive sun exposure?

3. Have you or someone you know ever eaten snake meat? What did it taste like?

4. If you've never eaten snake meat, would you be willing to try it? If so, research to find recipes using snake meat.

5. Glenda finds her first cattle drive "thrilling." What are some examples of modern-day experiences people find thrilling because they are unable to control the circumstances of the experience/thrill?

6. Why do some people seek and enjoy these thrilling experiences?

Comprehension Questions

1. What is used to give relief to Glenda's sunburned skin?

2. Why do Tobias, Emma, Zech, and the other members of the cattle company not find the grazing experiences thrilling?

3. Why do the MacIveys have no more right to the salty marsh grass than the men who force them to go elsewhere?

4. What vital part of Emma's personality emerges each time the family is threatened?

5. Why does Emma tell Glenda that more and more conflicts between cattlemen will occur as time passes?

6. Why do Emma and Glenda generate the reaction they receive when the men see them in "britches"?

7. What effective threat does Emma use to stop the comments the men make about her and Glenda's new clothes?

8. Why does Emma frown when Glenda mounts Ishmael?

9. What are Zech's reasons for building the cabin in Punta Rassa?

10. Why does Glenda want a horse of her own?

11. Why is the cattle company ambushed?

12. What do both Zech and Glenda lose in the attack?

13. How does Tobias's indifferent attitude to money leave the MacIvey Cattle Company vulnerable to attack?

14. Who does Zech blame for the death of the baby?

15. How does the loss of his daughter affect Zech?

Post-reading Activities

1. Complete/discuss teacher-selected Comprehension Questions.

2. Draw a "before" picture of Emma and Glenda in their dresses and an "after" picture in their new jeans, denim shirts, and boots. Include Glenda's black felt hat and red pony tail.

3. Have student volunteers dress up and model the "before" and "after" outfits of Emma and Glenda.

4. Make cardboard paper dolls of Emma and Glenda. Use paper to design and create the "before" and "after" clothes of Emma and Glenda.

Chapter 26

Vocabulary/Slang

cantered, sloughs, quest, ladled, stallion, mare, chickees

Pre-reading Activities

1. Locate the Ten Thousand Islands on a map of Florida.

2. Determine why the Ten Thousand Islands was an excellent refuge for the Confederate deserters and outlaws who once settled there.

Comprehension Questions

1. Tobias's citrus grove is described as "trees covered with balls of gold." Why is that description a metaphor?

2. Why does Zech return to the Seminole village?

3. Which particular Seminole does Zech recall as he rides south?

4. Besides the American government, who else have the Seminoles had difficulty with?

5. Read the conversation between Tawanda and Zech on pages 24 and 25. How do Tawanda and Zech feel about each other after the passage of so many years since their first meeting?

6. Zech's "other world seemed far away." What "world" is the author referring to?

Post-reading Activity

1. Complete/discuss teacher-selected Comprehension Questions.

Chapter 27

Vocabulary/Slang

"You deef?," squatters, dredges, land "development/developers," carcasses, range war, landlord, deed (relating to land), assets, diversification of assets

Pre-reading Activities

1. Examine the open-range ranching map found in the *Atlas of Florida* and examine the maps found there to determine how the open range was impacted by the citrus and phosphate industries.

2. How are the plants, animals, insects, and land of an ecosystem impacted when the land is dredged and drained for development?

3. After learning of the loss of more open range, Tobias decides to diversify his assets. What does that mean? Why is the diversification of assets an important and smart move for an entrepreneur?

Comprehension Questions
1. How does their baby's name indicate that Glenda has "opened a previously unknown world" to Zech?

2. How does Tobias learn that land he previously had free access to is now owned by someone?

3. How much did Hamilton Disston pay per acre for the land?

4. What new industries are taking control of the once-open range?

5. What plan does Zech have to keep more of the MacIvey land open to grazing?

Post-reading Activities
1. Complete/discuss teacher-selected Comprehension Questions.

2. Add the name of Zech and Glenda's son, Solomon MacIvey, to the MacIvey family tree.

3. Research the life of the Florida developer, Hamilton Disston.

4. What role did Hamilton Disston play in the development of the city of Tarpon Springs, Florida?

5. Prepare questions to interview native Floridians to record their memories and their reactions to the changes they have seen and experienced locally and in our state. Select natives who range from young people to the elderly. Be prepared to share your interviews with the class.

6. Invite local land developers of business and residential property to speak to the class. Brainstorm to prepare questions prior to their visit.

7. Invite to speak to the class officials of government and private agencies who are entrusted with and committed to protecting the land, its plants, animals, and waterways. Brainstorm to prepare questions prior to their visit.

Chapter 28

Vocabulary/Slang
way of life, ingrained, frontier

Pre-reading Activity
Research to determine how many acres and how many square miles make up Disney World in Orlando, Florida.

Comprehension Questions
1. How much land has Zech purchased?

2. How does the amount of land purchased by Zech compare with the number of acres that make up Disney World?

3. What does Zech plan to do that would stop open grazing on MacIvey land?

4. In what area of Florida does Zech believe his future would lie?

5. What does this belief mean?

6. What decision does Skillit make on behalf of his five sons?

7. Why does Skillit not have a last name?

8. What does Tobias mean when he tells Emma, "It's breaking up, Emma"?

9. List the events Tobias is recalling when he describes the time he has shared with Emma as "it's sure been something while it lasted"?

Post-reading Activities

1. Complete/discuss teacher-selected Comprehension Questions.

2. Research the Florida citrus industry to determine approximately how much Tobias could earn in today's market by owning 300 acres of productive orange groves.

3. Create a timeline of major events in the lives of the MacIvey family up to Chapter 28. Include artwork depicting these events.

Chapter 29

Vocabulary/Slang

quinine, breech loader gun, phosphate, speculators, land reclamation

Pre-reading Activities

1. Locate the date 1892 on the map in the front of the book.

2. Examine the map of Florida's railroad routes from 1865 to 1935 in the *Atlas of Florida*.

3. Read the section in the *Atlas of Florida* entitled "Phosphate Mining" and examine the map.

4. Read "The Stormy Origins of the Phosphate Industry" in *Florida's Past, Volume 3*.

Comprehension Questions

1. How are the cattle shipped from Punta Rassa to Cuba?

2. What solution does Glenda envision to avoid the drives to Punta Rassa?

3. What problems does Zech anticipate with the end of open-range grazing?

4. How old is Grampy?

5. How does the cattle company produce homegrown cows?

6. How are the homegrown cows different from wild cows?

7. Why are the cows oblivious to the danger of the locomotive?

8. What non-human object does Tobias "kill" with the breech loader?

9. What is land reclamation and why was there no such thing when the phosphate industry began in the state of Florida?

10. Do humans have the "inborn instinct" described by Zech on page 41? Explain your answer.

11. Why does Zech admire the animals' ability to "leave something for tomorrow"?

12. Why can't humans share without conflict when they have a need which is dependent on their mutual survival?

Post-reading Activities

1. Complete/discuss teacher-selected Comprehension Questions.

2. Research what "trouble was brewing" in Cuba in 1892 and how that trouble led to the Spanish-American War in 1898.

3. Research the historical significance of Tampa, Florida, during the Spanish-American War.

4. Research the growth of railroads in Florida and their role in the development of industry in the state.

5. Research the availability of passenger rail service in your area for a class train ride.

6. Search for older members of your community who have retired from the railroad. Invite them to the classroom to speak or have a student conduct a personal interview which would be reported to the class.

7. Find a picture of a steam-powered locomotive with a cowcatcher.

8. Research the role of the phosphate industry in the state of Florida. Include information regarding government-enforced land reclamation.

Chapter 30

Vocabulary/Slang
market price, egret plumes, cantered, seller's commission, buying on credit, riffraff, katydids, land survey

Pre-reading Activities

1. Pinpoint the area south of Lake Okeechobee on a map of Florida.

2. Locate a picture of Jacob Summerlin in the *Florida Portrait*.

3. Research the impact Summerlin had on the economic development of Florida.

4. Pinpoint the proximity of the Ten Thousand Islands to the area south of Lake Okeechobee.

5. In *Florida's Past, Volume 2* read "An Eyewitness to Shangri-la."

Comprehension Questions

1. What is the point of Jacob Summerlin's humorous comment to Zech on page 43?

2. Why is storing the gold doubloons a problem for the MacIveys?

3. Why don't they put the gold in a bank for safekeeping?

4. What other perishable products besides cheese would the store keeper not be able to stock for customers?

5. How would people living out in the scrub get these products?

6. Which salad dressing contains green/blue cheese mold?

7. Why are the feathers "growing out of a bird's rear" valuable?

8. Why is Zech unconcerned about leaving $9,000 in his saddlebags when he goes inside the store?

9. What is the purpose of a deed for land ownership?

10. How does Tawanda look when Zech sees her?

11. How many years have passed since Zech last saw Tawanda?

12. From whom does Toby inherit his riding ability?

13. Who does Tawanda name their son after?

14. What two promises does Tawanda request of Zech?

15. Why do you think she wants to keep the birth of their son secret from the world outside the village?

16. What would be your reaction if your mother suddenly introduced you to an unknown man who was your father?

17. What is Toby's reaction to Tawanda's revelation?

18. Describe the gifts Zech gives his son.

19. Who does Zech think the "bad men" from the Ten Thousand Islands may be?

20. What in Zech's behavior indicates that he is eager to return to Punta Rassa?

Post-reading Activities

1. Complete/discuss teacher-selected Comprehension Questions.

2. Compare the sixty thousand acres of land south of Lake Okeechobee purchased by Zech with the size of Disney World.

3. Draw a picture of what Toby might look like using the physical descriptions of Tawanda and Zech. Compare your drawings with the drawings of your classmates.

5. Research the murder of Guy Bradley, the Audubon Society's first law enforcement agent in the Everglades of Florida.

6. Locate pictures of bird plume feather hats from the late 1800s and early 1900s.

7. Create stylish hats which were popular from the late 1800s and early 1900s. Model your hats in a classroom fashion show.

Chapter 31

Vocabulary/Slang

fretted, kneaded the dough

Comprehension Questions

1. Approximately how many years have Tobias and Emma been married?

2. Why does Emma wait until the stew or roasted game is done before putting the biscuit dough into the Dutch oven for baking?

3. What physical ailment do Emma's symptoms indicate?

4. What do the three popping sound of Tobias's whip and the firing of both barrels of his shotgun indicate to the hunters?

5. Why does Zech feel it is necessary to bury Emma where they camped?

6. Why is cypress a better wood for a coffin than pine?

7. What does it mean "to take someone for granted"?

8. What will be Tobias's strongest memory of Emma?

9. What will be Zech's strongest memory of his mother?

10. What does the saying "happy sailing" mean?

11. Because there are no professional funeral services available, what funeral procedures do the family members have to assume to prepare Emma for burial?

Post-reading Activities

1. Complete/discuss teacher-selected Comprehension Questions.

2. Draw a picture of Emma as a young woman when we are first introduced to her in 1858 in Volume One and draw another picture of how she may have looked the year of her death in 1893. Compare your drawing with the drawings of your classmates.

3. Fold a piece of notebook paper in half lengthwise. List the admirable characteristics Emma possessed on the left side of your paper and write the name of a person/persons you know who has/have/had those same characteristics.

4. Order biscuits from your school cafeteria. Ask a volunteer to deliver the biscuits to the classroom dressed like Emma in period clothing.

5. Make Grandma Doris Mizell Drop Biscuits using one c. self-rising flour, 1/2 c. milk, and 3 T. mayonnaise. Bake at 375 degrees until brown. Yield approximately 9 biscuits. Grandma Doris and Grandpa Nathaniel Mizell were lifelong residents of Live Oak, Florida.

Chapter 32

Vocabulary/Slang

jest, barbed wire, adjacent, denim, invigorated, exhilaration, corn pone, "funning me," eerie, fodder, frail, flushed face, forlorn, foreboding, somber, lush, rations, dire, itinerant preacher

Pre-reading Activities

1. Pinpoint the location of the date 1895 on the map in the front of the book.

2. Describe the most beautiful snowfall you have ever seen. Bring in pictures to share.

3. Is your mother's personality similar to your grandmother's on your father's side of the family? If so, in what way are their personalities similar?

4. Is your father's personality similar to your grandfather's on your mother's side of the family? If so, in what way are they similar?

5. What temperature is freezing?

6. Describe a climatic disaster you have experienced.

7. If you have done so, describe your reaction to using a *real* outhouse. (Port-A-Potties don't count.)

8. What does sitting at the head of the table imply for the person who sits there?

9. Who sits at the head of the table in your home?

10. Is this position ever given up for another family member? If so, explain why.

Comprehension Questions

1. How does Zech plan to change the grazing habits of the cattle?

2. What personality characteristics do Emma and Glenda share?

3. How much of the orange groves are left to harvest?

4. How will a prolonged freeze affect the fruit?

5. What else besides oranges are affected by the freeze?

6. Why are the tree limbs falling from the trees?

7. Do you think Zech could have stopped Tobias from checking on the orange trees if he had "nailed the door shut"?

8. What is meant by Zech's promise to Tobias that he will "put it all back"?

9. In the first sentence on page 77 Glenda says, "We'll do whatever we have to do." Who does this sound like?

10. Why is it now Zech's duty to say "last words" for Tobias?

Post-reading Activities

1. Complete/discuss teacher-selected Comprehension Questions.

2. Draw a picture of the barbed wire fences enclosing the MacIvey homestead, land, and cattle.

3. Research the range wars which have occurred over the use of barbed wire on ranches and farms throughout the United States.

4. Invite local citrus growers or family members of citrus growers to speak to the class about the positives and negatives of growing citrus trees.

5. Research the evolution of the citrus industry in the state of Florida. Include the economic importance of citrus to the state and the effect of imported fruit on the industry.

6. Find pictures and read accounts of the freezes of 1894 and 1895.

7. Watch the videotape *Citrus Legacy,* available through the local PBS station in Orlando, Florida, which recounts the history of central Florida's most successful citrus-growing families.

8. Draw a picture of the MacIvey homestead covered with snow and ice. Include the house, citrus groves, trees and animals.

9. Bring a variety of citrus fruits for the class to sample. Check with local growers/distributors who may offer samples without charge.

10. Research citrus crate art/advertising. Have the students create citrus crate ads for the MacIvey Citrus Company and/or a citrus company using their last name.

Chapter 33

Vocabulary/Slang

dumbfounded, grieve, vowed

Pre-reading Activity

Pinpoint the location of Lake George on a map of Florida.

Comprehension Questions

1. Why are the landowners now selling their land so cheaply?

2. Who comes to pay respects to Tobias?

3. What does Zech learn of Tawanda?

4. Why are the Seminoles glad part of Zech is Seminole?

5. What vow does Zech make to himself?

Post-reading Activities

1. Complete/discuss teacher-selected Comprehension Questions.

2. Write an obituary honoring the life of Tobias.

Chapter 34

Vocabulary/Slang

revelers, parasols, clapboard houses, three-piece vested suits, Bowler hats, knickerbockers, prisms, boarding houses, suites, repulsive, gorging

Pre-reading Activities

1. Read the text in the *Atlas of Florida* that describes the growth of tourism in the state and examine the map that shows the railroad routes and hotels built by Henry Flagler and H. B. Plant.

2. Trace the route of the barefoot mailman who walked from Palm Beach to Miami to deliver the mail.

3. Find a picture of a Bowler hat.

4. Look at the picture of the golfers dressed in knickerbockers on page 175 of *Florida Portrait.*

Comprehension Questions

1. Describe the impact of development on birds, alligators, and garfish.

2. Why do today's beachgoers avoid sea turtle nesting sites?

3. Why was the Royal Poinciana such an unusual hotel for its time and location?

4. Compare the total number of guest rooms in Flagler's Royal Poinciana hotel with the Disney World Contemporary Resort, which contains 1008 rooms, and the Animal Kingdom Lodge, which contains 1293 rooms.

5. What is the correct spelling and pronunciation of the name of the man Zech refers to as "Ed-sun"?

6. What was the name of this inventor's creation that produced music?

7. Why would this invention have been so exciting for the people living in the late 1800s?

8. Describe the latest, most technically advanced device for listening to music.

9. How does this device compare with its earliest counterpart?

10. How many times more expensive is a room at the Royal Poinciana than a one-night stay at the boarding house in Punta Rassa?

11. What is the "indoor outhouse"?

12. Why is Zech repulsed by Palm Beach?

13. How does Sol demonstrate his ability as a young entrepreneur?

14. How does Sol conduct business in a manner that Tobias and Zech would not?

15. After buying the orange trees, what do the MacIveys do to avoid carrying the trunk of gold coins back to the hammock?

16. How many acres of trees does Zech intend to plant?

17. Why will the price of land increase with the introduction of the railroad?

18. Why is Zech's advice to Sol regarding thinking and talking in front of his mother good advice? Explain your answer.

19. What is today's place name location of the land purchased by Zech and Sol?

20. Why was Sol's choice of land a good investment?

Post-reading Activities

1. Complete/discuss teacher-selected Comprehension Questions.

2. Research the successful efforts of Henry Flagler to introduce tourism into the state of Florida.

3. As described on page 86, draw a picture of the stores and how the women and men looked as they strolled along the main street of Palm Beach.

4. Locate a photo and research the history of the Royal Poinciana Hotel.

5. Research to find information about the winter home of Thomas Alva Edison in Fort Myers, Florida.

6. Locate a picture of the "box that produced music" and describe how it worked.

7. Research the role of Julia Tuttle in the development of Miami.

8. Read "When Mail Carriers Were Trailblazers" from *Florida's Past, Volume 2,* which describes the perils of the mailmen who walked barefoot to deliver the mail along the early Florida east coast.

Chapter 35

Vocabulary/Slang

rustling, rampant, beeves, gunslingers, cut of my britches, whiskey still, poultice

Pre-reading Activities

1. Locate the date 1896 on the map in the front of the book.

2. Locate the city of Arcadia, which is located in DeSoto County, on a map of Florida.

3. Locate "down south of Punta Rassa, at the edge of the Ten Thousand islands" on a map of Florida, which is the location of the outlaws' hideout.

4. Describe a modern-day circumstance in which the citizens might be forced to "take the law into their own hands."

5. What consequences would those citizens assume for their action?

Comprehension Questions

1. Why does Zech send Frog to Arcadia?

2. What does Frog's description of the citizenry of Arcadia imply about the organization of the town government?

3. In consideration of the risks, do you agree or disagree with Zech's decision to go after the rustlers? Explain your answer.

4. Why will Glenda be thankful that Sol disobeyed and followed his father to the rustlers' camp?

5. What was the Punta Rassa doctor's plan to treat Zech's foot?

6. Why did the doctor pour whiskey into the open wound?

7. Was Zech's solution to the care of his foot injury successful?

8. Why is it important for Sol to know that Zech had a loving relationship with Tawanda before he married Glenda?

9. How is the Seminole resting place for the dead different from how non-Seminole people put their loved ones to rest?

10. What is the significance of burial markers?

11. Considering how they interact during Zech's recovery, what conclusion can you draw about the relationship between Toby and Sol?

Post-reading Activities

1. Complete/discuss teacher-selected Comprehension Questions.

2. Draw a picture of the rough town of Arcadia as described by Frog on page 104. For reference, use Frederic Remington's drawings of Cracker Cowboys and the photos of old Florida towns from the *Florida Portrait.*

Chapter 36

Vocabulary/Slang

cantankerous, gnarled

Pre-reading Activities

1. Locate a picture and description of a Brahma bull.

2. Compare the size of Zech's 8,000 acres of orange grove with the size of Disney World.

3. Considering the businesses he will inherit from his father, would Sol necessarily need a formal education? Explain your answer.

Comprehension Questions

1. List the four advantages the Brahma bull has over the Florida cattle.

2. What are the advantages for Zech to ship the oranges north rapidly by rail rather than by boat?

3. Refer to Chapter 27 to determine Sol's age in Chapter 36.

4. What proposal does Glenda make for Sol's educational future?

5. How does the bull prove to be more dangerous than the MacIvey Cattle Company realize?

6. Why is Zech's comparison of loving dogs and loving a woman as being the same kind of love, not an offense to the memory of Glenda?

7. Do you agree or disagree with Zech's advice to Sol about never getting "tied up with a woman"? Explain your answer.

8. Who does Frog expect to see and speak with after his death?

9. Why does Zech ask for God's forgiveness for buying the bull?

10. Did he need to ask for forgiveness? Explain your answer.

Post-reading Activities

1. Complete/discuss teacher-selected Comprehension Questions.

2. Draw a picture of the MacIvey grave site after the burial of Glenda and Frog.

Chapter 37

Vocabulary/Slang

thunderhead, polled, currycomb, surplus, grieve

Pre-reading Activities

1. Locate the date 1905 on the map in the front of the book.

2. Find the location of the 70,000 acres Zech purchases that stretch "from the lake's southwest shore to the edge of the cypress swamp" on a map.

3. Locate a picture of a Hereford bull.

4. Research to find the current cost of a mature Hereford bull.

Comprehension Questions

1. How is the Hereford bull different from the Brahma?

2. What two changes are made to the MacIvey Cattle Company after the last drive of 1898?

3. How much land does Zech now own? How does this compare with the size of Disney World?

4. What fraction of the breed keeps the cows from being 100% Hereford?

5. Why does Zech buy the additional 70,000 acres?

6. Who are the last blood-related survivors of the MacIvey family?

7. Approximately how old would Skillet MacIvey's children be?

8. What do you think has happened to them since leaving the MacIveys?

Chapter 38

Vocabulary/Slang

bandanna

Pre-reading Activity

Locate the date 1908 on the map in the front of the book.

Comprehension Questions

1. Refer to Chapter 27 to determine Sol's age in 1908.

2. Why does Sol feel compelled to leave the MacIvey cattle ranch and orange groves?

3. Do you agree with Jessie that the memories people leave when they have passed away are more important than objects? Explain your answer.

4. Where is Sol storing the trunks of money?

5. Do you consider Sol emotionally weaker than Tobias or Zech because he wants to leave the homestead? Explain your answer.

6. Besides death, why are there no more "old-time crackers" in Florida?

Post-reading Activities

1. Complete/discuss teacher-selected comprehension questions.

2. Draw a picture of Sol with a thought cartoon balloon picturing what he saw in his mind's eye as described on page 138, paragraph 2.

Chapter 39

Vocabulary/Slang

tracts, sloughs, dredges, soot, knickers

Pre-reading Activities

1. Locate a picture of a foot-pedal Singer sewing machine.

2. Find and read the section in the *Atlas of Florida* about the destruction of the Everglades due to agricultural development.

3. Read "Trailblazers of the Great Swamp" from *Florida's Past, Volume 2* for an account of the building of the Tamiami Trail across the Everglades.

4. Reread the vivid description of the custard-apple forest as described in Volume One page 193, paragraph 6 to page 195, paragraph 6.

5. Read page 139, paragraph 1. Describe how Zech's reaction to the land would have been different from Sol's?

6. Reread page 98, paragraph 10. What does young Sol hear the land agent, Mr. Potter, tell Zech?

7. Why is "soil so black that it looked like soot" more fertile than white, sandy soil?

8. How has the attitude toward nature, as verbalized by Sol on page 144, paragraph 2, led to extinct and endangered designations for certain species of plants and animals?

Comprehension Questions

1. How does Sol want to "transform the land"?

2. What is the name of the third company developed by a MacIvey?

3. Reread page 140, paragraph 2. Describe how you felt when you read this paragraph describing the destruction of the custard-apple forest.

4. According to Minnie, why is it important for Sol to have sons?

5. Why does Toby feel that God is represented in a swamp but not in a tomato field?

6. After Toby confronts him, does Sol regret destroying the custard-apple forest?

7. What does Sol's drive into West Palm Beach indicate about his concern for animals?

8. As an adult at the Royal Poinciana, how does Sol face discrimination?

9. After Sol repeats his name to the desk clerk, do you believe Sol will keep his promise to him? Explain your answer.

10. Bonnie's father is Irish. How does Sol describe his ancestry?

11. How does Bonnie's response that she and her father "got a garden too" indicate that she has no idea who Sol MacIvey is and what he does for a living?

12. Why is Bonnie so willing to go with Sol?

13. Do you agree with Sol that Bonnie is "the kind of girl my mamma would like"? Explain your answer.

14. How is Sol's first encounter with a young woman who is not a family member indicative of his poorly developed social skills?

15. How does Sol's encounter with Bonnie compare with Zech's first encounter of Glenda at the frolic?

Post-reading Activities

1. Complete/discuss teacher-selected Comprehension Questions.

2. Locate a picture of a Model-T Ford. Draw a picture of Sol in the manner he was driving the Model-T from Belle Glade to West Palm Beach.

3. Draw a picture of Bonnie or cut out a picture of someone in a magazine who looks like Bonnie as described on page 147, paragraph 9.

4. Draw a before-and-after picture of the custard-apple forest.

Chapter 40

Vocabulary/Slang

flivver, clerical work, percentage basis, bookkeeper, rambling

Pre-reading Activities

1. Use a map of Florida to trace Sol's drive from his home south of Lake Okeechobee to the homestead. Find the location of the town of Basinger.

2. Locate a picture of a Ford Model-T truck to see the model Sol used to haul the remaining gold-filled trunks from the homestead to his home.

Comprehension Questions

1. Refer to the date from Chapter 39 to determine how long Bonnie and Sol have remained friends.

2. Refer to Chapter 27 to determine how old Sol is in Chapter 40.

3. Why is Sol so eager to return to the homestead?

4. Describe Bonnie's relationship with Sol.

5. How has the homestead changed since Sol's last visit?

6. What is left of the original homestead?

7. Even though he has never met Sol, how is Donovan able to draw the conclusion that the angry man pointing the Winchester at him is Sol MacIvey?

8. Are the profits from the "three hundred acres of good land where that hammock was" that important to Sol?

9. When Sol confronts Donovan, what is likely to happen if Bonnie does not intervene?

10. Reread the description of Emma's cook stove from Volume One, page 136, paragraph 2. Why is the cook stove so important to Sol?

11. When he compares his destruction of the custard-apple forest with Donovan's disregard for the MacIvey homestead, what does Sol realize about himself?

12. Why does Sol believe that "nothing in this whole stinking world lasts forever"?

13. How do we know that Sol has not shared any of the history of the MacIvey family with Bonnie?

14. Why do you think Sol has kept this history to himself?

Post-reading Activities

1. Complete/discuss teacher-selected Comprehension Questions.

2. Place students into groups and make a Ford Model-T from a kit.

3. Draw a before-and-after picture of the homestead as described in the chapter.

Chapter 41

Vocabulary/Slang

skiff, mangrove swamp, frock coat, stovepipe hat, walk-in vault, great Florida Boom, commercial area, residential area, muckland

Pre-reading Activities

1. Locate the cities of Miami and Miami Beach on a map of Florida. Where are these cities in relation to Sol's Lake Okeechobee home?

2. Examine the photos in Chapters 9 and 10 in *Florida Portrait* to determine how the tourist industry, population growth, and land development affected the state from 1900 to the 1920s.

3. Research the economic depression of the 1930s in the United States and its effect upon the personal and business finances of Florida's citizens.

4. Locate a photo of Henry Flagler. Does he look like a multimillionaire? Explain your answer.

5. Read the following:
From *Florida's Past, Volume 1* read "Mother Tuttle of Miami," "DuPont Rescues Florida's Busted Banks," "The Bohemian Birth of Coconut Grove," "The Rise and Fall of Carl Fisher's Miami Beach," "The 'Binder Boys' Burst the Great Boom Battle," and "The Flagler Divorce Law Furor."

From *Florida's Past, Volume 2* read "When Greed Infected Rogue Florida," and "When Anti-Semitism Plagued Miami Beach."

From *Florida's Past, Volume 3,* read: "Miami's Heritage: A Doctor Remembered," "Mr. Jiggs Opens the Swamp Country," "When Land Was Sold by the Gallon," and "Carrie Nation Dries Up Miami."

6. Considering that five stacks of $20,000 (equaling $100,000) stands 6 feet tall, determine how large Sol's vault would have

to be to hold $81,000,000. The size of a bill is 2.5 inches wide and 6 inches long. (The largest bill denomination local banks carry today is $100.)

Comprehension Questions

1.   How old is Sol in 1924?

2.   How long have Sol and Bonnie been friends?

3.   How do we know that Julia Tuttle was finally able to successfully communicate her idea of the market potential of Miami to Henry Flagler?

4.   Why is Sol's Miami property increasing in value?

5.   Why does Sol have his Miami home built with foot-thick concrete walls and iron grills across the windows?

6.   How does "banking by trunk" save the MacIvey fortune during the Great Depression of the 1930s?

7.   List the names of the four businesses started by members of the MacIvey family.

8.   How many acres of land does Sol own in Miami?

9.   How many 70' x 100' lots does Sol create from a 208' x 208' acre?

10.   Why is the Miami Beach acreage more valuable than Sol's other property?

11.   Describe Tobias's likely reaction if he were alive to see the eighty million dollars in Sol's vault.

Post-reading Activities

1.   Complete/discuss teacher-selected Comprehension Questions.

2.   Research to find information about the first trip of Flagler's overseas railroad between Miami and Key West. Pretend you are a passenger. Write a letter or newspaper article describing your ride. Include a picture.

3.   Draw a picture of Sol's unusual Miami home.

4.   Write and illustrate a newspaper, magazine, or billboard advertisement encouraging potential buyers of the value and beauty of owning Florida real estate in the 1920s. Your ad must reflect the advertising styles of that period.

Chapter 42

Vocabulary/Slang

frenzied, economic recovery, pollen, cannibal, eerie, omen, leaden skies, gusts, gospel hymns, dike

Pre-reading Activities

1.   Research modern-day methods of hurricane prediction and tracking.

2. Use a hurricane tracking chart to track the movement of a fictitious hurricane by marking daily longitude and latitude coordinates posted by your teacher on your hurricane tracking chart.

3. Research hurricane preparedness and recovery.

4. Divide the class into family groups. Have half the family groups research preparedness and recovery in the event of evacuation. Have the other family groups research preparedness and recovery for remaining at home during the storm. Have the family groups report their findings to the class.

5. Contact local Emergency Preparedness governmental agencies for hurricane-related videotapes, compact discs, handouts, and the possibility of scheduling a guest speaker.

6. Research accounts of the 1928 hurricane in which a dike surrounding part of Lake Okeechobee broke resulting in the drowning of over two thousand people.

7. Read Florida writer Zora Neale Hurston's fictional account of the 1928 hurricane in Chapter 18 of *Their Eyes Were Watching God*.

8. Research the history of hurricanes which have occurred in the state of Florida.

Comprehension Questions

1. How old is Sol in Chapter 42?

2. How long have Bonnie and Sol remained friends?

3. Why do you think Bonnie is willing to give up the emotional security of marriage for the physical security Sol provides?

4. Why do you think Sol is unwilling to give Bonnie the financial and emotional security of marriage? Why do you think his attitude toward marriage is different from the attitudes of Tobias and Zech in this matter?

5. Why do Sol and Bonnie leave Miami?

6. What tragedy ends Sol's ability to earn profit from the sale of his Miami property?

7. By recalling the MacIvey reaction to tragedy, how does Sol profit from the tragedy?

8. Of what is the house at Lake Okeechobee constructed?

9. List the six signs Sol and Bonnie observe that signal the coming of a great storm?

10. Why doesn't Sol take the advice he believes Toby would have given him considering the signs?

11. What is the bad omen associated with hearing a hooting owl?

12. What consequence of the hurricane has the greatest impact on the safety of Sol and Bonnie?

13. What is the "one big round area of peaceful sky surrounded by spinning madness" which creates the lull in the storm?

14. What impact does the second phase of the hurricane have on the house that the first phase did not?

15. How will Sol's grief be different from the grief suffered by Tobias and Zech?

Post-reading Activities

1. Complete/discuss teacher-selected Comprehension Questions.

2. Write a newspaper article describing the tragedy in Okeechobee from the 1928 hurricane.

3. Write an account of an interview with a fictitious survivor of the tragedy.

4. Draw a picture of the house as described on page 165, paragraph 3.

5. Draw a picture of the devastation described in the last paragraph on page 166 and on page 167.

6. In order to create an audio history, onduct an interview with someone who has experienced a Florida hurricane.

Chapter 43

Vocabulary/Slang

massive, four-inch spiked-heeled shoes, hard cash, Depression, war bond drives, USO, tract houses, St. Augustine lawns, scrounge, phantom, custom-made, tailor, day of reckoning, catchword

Pre-reading Activities

1. Locate and compare photos of Miami and Miami Beach in the 1950s and the present.

2. Give your impression of the area if you have lived in or visited Miami or Miami Beach.

3. Locate and compare statistics which indicate the population trends of Miami and Miami Beach in the 1950s and the present.

4. Find Key Biscayne, which was the location of Sol's mansion, on a map of the Miami area.

5. On a map of Florida locate the following cities, which Sol developed: Hollywood, Fort Lauderdale, Pompano, Boca Raton, and Lake Worth. Give your impression if you have lived in or visited these cities.

Comprehension Questions

1. How old is Sol in Chapter 43?

2. How many years have passed since the Lake Okeechobee tragedy?

3. What award does Sol receive?

4. Why is he selected for this award?

5. The woman interviewing Sol congratulates him and says, "You certainly deserve it for all you've done for the state." What does her statement imply?

6. Do you agree with her implication? Justify your answer.

7. Why does Sol make up his family history?

8. List four consequences of building the dikes and drainage canals to the Big Upper Swamp and the Everglades.

9. How is Sol's reaction to Bonnie's death different from the reaction of Tobias and Zech to the deaths of Emma and Glenda?

10. Of what materials is the Lake Okeechobee home rebuilt?

11. What assets does Sol use to begin the MacIvey State Bank?

12. How did the cost of land in the 1930s compare with the selling price of land in the 1920s?

13. Does Sol find another companion to replace Bonnie?

14. How does Sol prove to be a philanthropist during World War II?

15. What is the sixth MacIvey business created to fulfill a promise sworn by Sol forty-three years earlier?

16. Explain the statement, he served "as boss of the MacIvey empire in name only."

17. Why does Sol go to the ceremony to honor him dressed in late - 1800s—style clothing?

18. Describe how Tobias, Emma, Zech, Glenda, and Toby would react to the description of the MacIveys as "one of Florida's most important families" and Sol as " a man who played a major role in conquering the wilderness and bringing civilization and progress to Florida."

19. Why does Sol correct the audience's belief that it was he who "conquered the Florida wilderness"?

20. Do you agree with Sol's comment that he is "the least" of the MacIveys?

21. Why does Sol consider himself "stupid" and the members of the audience "greedy"?

22. Describe your reaction to Sol's statement that "Progress ain't reversible."

23. If he were to see the current development of the state of Florida, how would Sol react?

24. How do you think the audience reacted after Sol left the ceremony?

25. How effective do you think Sol's speech was in convincing the developers to curb their destruction of the Florida environment?

Post-reading Activities

1. Complete/discuss teacher-selected Comprehension Questions.

2. Draw a picture of Sol seated behind his massive mahogany desk in his corporate executive office atop the MacIvey State Bank.

3. Draw pictures of the Big Cypress Swamp and the Everglades before and after Lake Okeechobee was diked and the drainage canals were cut.

4. Draw a before-and-after picture of the Okeechobee house.

5. Divide the class into two groups. Brainstorm with Group One about how modest, casual vacation homes on the water are constructed. Have this group draw what they think Sol's single-story "sturdy old cypress house at Lake Okeechobee" looked like. After comparing drawings, have the group build a model of the Lake Okeechobee cypress house using popsicle sticks and glue. The students can work in pairs to construct the various parts of the house such as the walls, roof, and floor. After they are completely dry, glue these portions of the house together.
    The second group will work on the rebuilt Okeechobee house, which was made "this time of concrete and steel." Brainstorm with Group Two about how the design of the second house would not reflect the casualness of a vacation home, but the anger Sol felt after losing Bonnie in the old cypress house. Have Group Two draw what they think the the concrete and steel Lake Okeechobee home would look like. After comparing drawings, assign the group to build the home of sugar cubes, representing concrete blocks, glued together to form the walls and floor. A "steel" roof can be made of a piece of aluminum foil.

6. Draw a picture of Sol dressed in the late 1800s black custom-made suit he wore to the ceremony to honor him.

7. Write a newspaper article for the *Miami Herald* describing the evening's events of the ceremony to honor Sol.

Chapter 44

Vocabulary/Slang

Rolls Royce, causeway, idly, decades, Seminole reservations, wildlife/environmental preserve

Pre-reading Activities

1. Locate 1968 on the map in the front of the book.

2. Read page 177, paragraph 2. How do the events from Florida's history as described by Sol trace the destruction of various people since Florida was settled?

3. Find the paragraphs and the chart and maps in the *Atlas of Florida* that describe the American Indian population of Florida. Note the location of Miami, the Tamiami Trail, and the Miccosukee Indian Reservation on the maps of the Reservation and Trust Lands.

4. Research why the influx of refugees from Latin America and the tensions between the black and white citizens of Miami resulted in riots during the summer of 1968.

5. If you have visited one of the Seminole Tribe of Florida Reservations, describe your experience.

Comprehension Questions

1. How old is Sol in 1968?

2. What is Sol's relationship with Arthur?

3. Why is Sol leaving the Key Biscayne mansion?

4. How has Miami changed since Sol first saw it?

5. Why is Sol not shocked by the Miami riot of 1968?

6. How long has it been since Sol has spoken with Toby since they last met in 1911?

7. What changes does Sol observe in the Seminole village as compared with the changes that have taken place in Miami?

8. Describe Toby Cypress.

9. If he was nine years old in 1892 when Zech first learned of him, how old is Toby in 1968?

10. How has Toby demonstrated the MacIvey family characteristic of responsibility and caring for others?

11. Why are Sol's requests of Toby unrealistic?

12. Why is it important for Sol and Toby to express their forgiveness and love for each other before they die?

13. Why doesn't Sol give his wealth to Toby's sons who have MacIvey blood?

14. When the car leaves the village, Sol does not look back. Why does he not take one last look at the village?

Post-reading Activities

1. Complete/discuss teacher-selected Comprehension Questions.
2. Draw Solomon and Toby as elderly men dressed in clothing and settings appropriate to their cultures.

3. Invite private and public preservation groups to speak to the class regarding their efforts to protect wildlife and habitats. Brainstorm to prepare questions before their visit.

3. Research to find examples of how citizens of all ages and occupations have worked to preserve and protect local and state habitats, historical natural areas, and historical landmarks.

4. Write a letter to the editor of your school newspaper, city newspaper, or prepare a speech encouraging the preservation of a local habitat or landmark.

Chapter 45

Vocabulary/Slang

logjam, carbon monoxide, weathered, automobile title, trust fund, cane-bottom rocker, frail

Pre-reading Activities

1. Use the date 1968 to find the location of the Zech and Glenda's cabin near Punta Rassa in the front of the book.

2. Pinpoint the location of Naples and the Caloosahatchee River on a map of Florida.

Comprehension Questions

1. Describe the impact of increased population and development on the once-pristine area south of Naples.

2. How has Sol protected the Punta Rassa acreage and cabin from development?

3. From whom does Sol inherit his health problem?

4. How does Sol show his appreciation for Arthur's thirty years of service?

5. Does Sol's impatient, tough response to Arthur's expressions of gratitude accurately reflect Sol's genuine feelings for his friend and employee of thirty years?

6. What was the origin of the "old board tacked to the wall with white faded letters" that read "The MacIvey Cattle Company"?

7. What MacIvey family history can you recall from the Winchesters and the ten-gauge double-barreled shotgun which are in the gun rack and the rusty branding iron placed next to them?

8. Why is it appropriate that Sol's final effort is to pop a whip?

9. List the people Sol recalls and the memory he recalls about them.

10. Why are Sol's last words "Where did it all go, Pappa?. . . Where did it all go?. . ."?

11. Read page 26, paragraph 2. Did Sol live up to the meaning of his name?

Post-reading Activities

1. Complete/discuss teacher-selected Comprehension Questions.

2. List the names of the major characters in the book. Pretend a movie of the book is being produced and you are in charge of selecting popular actors and actresses to perform in their roles. List the names of the actors and actresses you would choose.

3. How could the book have ended differently?

4. What could a sequel be about?

5. Use cardboard to recreate the MacIvey Cattle Company sign.

6. Draw Sol seated on the cypress bench beside the cabin porch imagining the members of the MacIvey family.

7. Write an obituary for Solomon MacIvey.

Sunshine State Standards

Studying *A Land Remembered* fulfills many benchmarks of the Sunshine State Standards for Social Studies and some for Science for the middle grades.

Social Studies Grades 6–8

A. Time, Continuity, and Change (History)

A.1.3   understands historical chronology and the historical perspective.

A.1.3.1 understands how patterns, chronology, sequencing (including cause and effect)and the identification of historical periods are influenced by frames of reference.

A.1.3.3 knows how to impose temporal structure on historical narratives.

A.4.3   understands U.S. history to 1880.

A.4.3.1 knows the factors involved in the development of cities, and industries (e.g., religious needs, the need for military protection, the need for a marketplace, changing spatial patterns, and geographical factors for location such as transportation and food supply).

A.4.3.2 knows the role of physical and cultural geography in shaping events in the United States (e.g. environmental and climatic influences on settlement of the colonies, the American Revolution, and the Civil War).

A.5.3   understands U.S. history from 1880 to the present day.

A.5.3.1 understands the role of physical and cultural geography in shaping events in the United States since 1880 (e.g., western settlement, immigration patterns, and urbanization).

A.5.3.2 understands ways that significant individuals and events influenced economic, social, and political systems in the United States after 1880.

A.5.3.3 knows the causes and consequences of urbanization that occurred in the United States after 1880 (e.g., causes such as industrialization; consequences such as poor living conditions in cities and employment conditions).

A.6.3   understands the history of Florida and its people.

A.6.3.1 understands how immigration and settlement patterns have shaped the history of Florida (e.g., American, Spanish, Minorcan, Cuban, Haitian, etc.).

A.6.3.2 knows the unique geographic and demographic characteristics that define Florida as a region.

A.6.3.3 knows how the environment of Florida has been modified by the values, traditions, and actions of various groups who have inhabited the state.

A.6.3.4 understands how the interactions of societies and cultures have influenced Florida's history.

A.6.3.5 understands how Florida has allocated and used resources and the consequences of those economic decisions.

B. People, Places, and Environments (Geography)

B.1.3   understands the world in spatial terms.

B.1.3.1 uses various map forms and other geographic representations, tools, and technologies to acquire, process, and report geographic information including patterns of land use, connections between places, and patterns and processes of migration and diffusion.

B.2.3   understands the interactions of people and the physical environment.

B.2.3.4 understands how the landscape and society change as a consequence of shifting from a dispersed to a concentrated settlement form.

C. Government and the Citizen

C.2.3   understands the role of the citizen in American democracy.

C.2.3.6 understands the importance of participation in community service, civic improvement, and political activities.

Science Grades 6–8
G. How Living Things Interact with Their Environment

G.2.3.1 knows that some resources are renewable and others are nonrenewable.

G.2.3.2 knows that all biotic and abiotic factors are interrelated and that if one factor is changed or removed, it impacts the availability of other resources within the system.

G.2.3.3 knows that a brief change in the limited resources of an ecosystem may alter the size of a population or the average size of individual organisms and that long-term change may result in the elimination of animal and plant populations inhabiting the earth.

G.2.3.4 understands that humans are a part of an ecosystem and their activities may deliberately or inadvertently alter the equilibrium in ecosystems.

Language Arts Grades 6–8
A. Reading

A.1.3.2 uses a variety of strategies to analyze words and text, draw conclusions, use context and word structure clues, and recognize organizational patterns.

A.2.3.1 determines the main idea or essential message in a text and identifies relevant details and facts and patterns of organization.

A.2.3.5 locates, organizes, and interprets written information for a variety of purposes, including classroom research, collaborative decision making, and performing a school or real-world task.

B. Writing

B.2.3.4 uses electronic technology including databases and software to gather information and communicate new knowledge.

C. Listening, Viewing, and Speaking

C.1.3.1 listens and uses information gained for a variety of purposes, such as gaining information from interviews, following directions, and pursuing a personal interest.

D. Language

D.1.3.1 understands that there are patterns and rules in semantic structure, symbols, sounds, and meanings conveyed through the English language.

D.1.3.4 understands that languages change over time.

Resources

Books

Adams, Alto Jr. and Lee Gramling. *A Florida Cattle Ranch*. Sarasota, Florida: Pineapple Press, 1998.

Burnett, Gene M. *Florida's Past: People and Events that Shaped the State Volume 1*. Sarasota, Florida: Pineapple Press, 1986.

Burnett, Gene M. *Florida's Past: People and Events that Shaped the State Volume 2*. Sarasota, Florida: Pineapple Press, 1988.

Burnett, Gene M. *Florida's Past: People and Events that Shaped the State Volume 3*. Sarasota, Florida: Pineapple Press, 1991.

Downs, Dorothy. *Patchwork: Seminole and Miccosukee Art and Activities*. Sarasota, Florida: Pineapple Press, 2005.

Fernald, Edward, and Elizabeth Purdum. *Atlas of Florida*. Tallahassee, Florida: University Press of Florida, 1992.

Florida's Vanishing Wildlife Coloring Book. Palm Harbor, Florida: Seaside Publishing.

Haase, Ronald. *Classic Cracker: Florida's Wood-Frame Vernacular Architecture*. Sarasota, Florida: Pineapple Press, 1992.

Hurston, Zora Neale. *Their Eyes Were Watching God*. New York: Perennial, 1998.

Lantz, Peggy, and Wendy Hale. *The Young Naturalist's Guide to Florida*. Sarasota, Florida: Pineapple Press, 1990.

Looper, Don. *Lament of the Cracker Cowboy*. Pebble Beach, California: Pebble Beach Press, 1998.

Lyons, Ernest. *My Florida*. New York: A. S. Barnes, 1969.

Maehr, David S., and Herbert Kale II. *Florida's Birds, 2nd Edition*. Sarasota, Florida: Pineapple Press, 2005.

Nelson, Gil. *The Trees of Florida: A Reference and Field Guide*. Sarasota, Florida: Pineapple Press, 1994.

O'Sullivan , Maurice, and Jack Lane, eds. *The Florida Reader: Visions of Paradise from 1530 to the Present*. Sarasota, Florida: Pineapple Press, 1991.

Ohr, Tim. *Florida's Fabulous Natural Places*. California: World Publications, 1998.

Rawlings, Marjorie Kinnan. *The Yearling*. New York: Scribner, 2002.

Rush, Beverly, and Lassie Wittman. *The Complete Book of Seminole Patchwork*. Mineola, New York: Dover Publications, 1994.

Shofner, Jerrell. *Florida Portrait: A Pictorial History of Florida*. Sarasota, Florida: Pineapple Press, 1990.

They Called It Florida. DeWitt, Inc. 4504 W. Elm St., Tampa, FL 33614. 813-885-1939. Other reasonably priced coloring books with Florida subject matter are also available.

Whitney, Ellie, Bruce Means, and Anne Rudloe. *Priceless Florida: Natural Ecosystems and Native Species*. Sarasota, Florida: Pineapple Press, 2004.

Williams, Winston. *Florida's Fabulous Trees*. California: World Publications, 1998.

Cracker Westerns:

Chapman, Herb and Muncy. *Wiregrass Country*. Sarasota, Florida: Pineapple Press, 1998.

Gramling, Lee. *Ghosts of the Green Swamp*. Sarasota, Florida: Pineapple Press, 1996.

Gramling, Lee. *Ninety-Mile Prairie*. Sarasota, Florida: Pineapple Press, 2002.

Gramling, Lee. *Riders of the Suwannee*. Sarasota, Florida: Pineapple Press, 1993.

Gramling, Lee. *Thunder on the St. Johns*. Sarasota, Florida: Pineapple Press, 1994.

Gramling, Lee. *Trail from St. Augustine*. Sarasota, Florida: Pineapple Press, 1993.

Tonyan, Rick. *Guns of the Palmetto Plains*. Sarasota, Florida: Pineapple Press, 1994.

Wilson, Jon. *Bridger's Run*. Sarasota, Florida: Pineapple Press, 1999.

Videotapes

Citrus Farming for Kids. National Resource Conservation Service. Available through Rainbow Communications, 1276 School Rd., Victor, NY 14564. 800-518-3276. Fax 585-742-3437. www.farmkidvid.com

The Honey Files. The National Honey Board, 309 Lashley St., Longmont, CO 80501-6045. 800-553-7162 or 303-776-2337.

Judge Platt: Tales of a Florida Cow-hunter. Available through UF/IFAS Extension Bookstore. 800-226-1764. www.ifasbooks.com.

If you enjoyed reading this book, here are some other fiction titles from Pineapple Press. To request a catalog or to place an order, write to Pineapple Press, P.O. Box 3889, Sarasota, Florida 34230, or call 1-800-PINEAPL (746-3275). Or visit our website at www.pineapplepress.com.

A Land Remembered by Patrick Smith. This well-loved, best-selling novel tells the story of three generations of the MacIveys, a Florida family battling the hardships of the frontier, and how they rise from a dirt-poor cracker life to the wealth and standing of real estate tycoons. (hb & pb)

A Land Remembered Student Edition by Patrick D. Smith. This best-selling novel is now available to young readers in two volumes. (hb & pb)

A Land Remembered Goes to School by Tillie Newhart and Mary Lee Powell. An elementary school teacher's manual, using *A Land Remembered* to teach language arts, social studies, and science, coordinated with the Sunshine State Standards of the Florida Department of Education. (pb)

The Spy Who Came In from the Sea by Peggy Nolan. In 1943 fourteen-year-old Frank Holleran sees an enemy spy land on Jacksonville Beach. First Frank needs to get people to believe him, and then he needs to stop the spy from carrying out his dangerous plans. Winner of the Sunshine State Young Reader's Award. (hb & pb)

Blood Moon Rider by Zack C. Waters. When his Marine father is killed in WWII, young Harley Wallace is exiled to the Florida cattle ranch of his bitter, badly scarred grandfather. The murder of a cowman and the disappearance of Grandfather Wallace leads Harley and his new friend Beth on a wild ride through the swamps and into the midst of a conspiracy of evil. (hb) (Available Spring 2006)

Escape to the Everglades by Edwina Raffa and Annelle Rigsby. Based on historical fact, this young adult novel tells the story of Will Cypress, a half-Seminole boy living among his mother's people during the Second Seminole War. He meets Chief Osceola and travels with him to St. Augustine. (hb) (Available Spring 2006)

Solomon by Marilyn Bishop Shaw. Young Solomon Freeman, and his parents, Moses and Lela, survive the Civil War, gain their freedom, and gamble their dreams, risking their very existence, on a homestead in the remote environs of north central Florida. (hb) (Available Spring 2006)